'TOENAILS'

BY **Dani Brown**

Brought to you from:

With an excerpt from Dani Brown's: "MY LOVELY WIFE"

pg. 88

Dani Brown

<u>MorbidbookS</u> Is A Grotesque Bizarro Ballet Where The Most Profane Things Occur. An Impious And Perverse Dwelling Of Dark Revulsion. A Cozy Cottage Where Torture Porn And Brutal Bible Tales Are Devised. A Quiet Place To Relax And Spin Tales Of Depravity And Wickedness. A Halfway House For The Disturbed Where Rules No Longer Apply. A Safe Haven For Deviant Serial Killers To Hatch Their Wretched Schemes. Far, Far Off The Reservation. Bring Your Pets. The Tasty Ones Are Always Welcome.

<u>WWW.MORBIDBOOKS.WORDPRESS.COM</u>

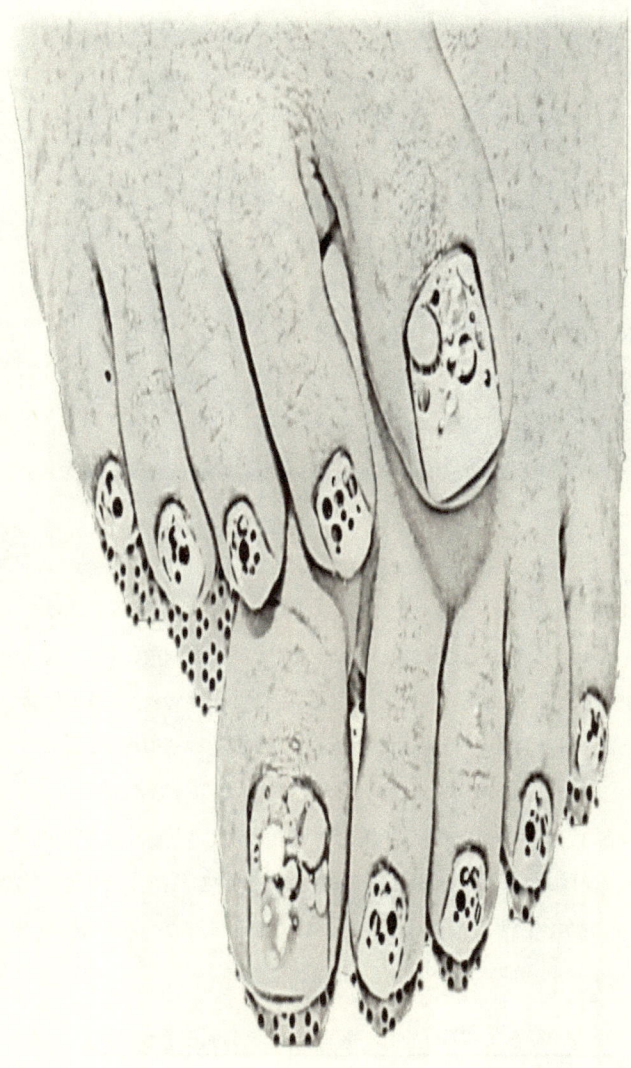

TOENAILS

ONE

Upon waking, the first thing to be considered before even the coffee was put on, was how to score enough toenails to see me through the day. They were like crack to me; only more addictive and typically not as foul smelling.

Some people need coffee to get going in the mornings. Others need smack to chase night demons out of their veins. I required toenail clippings, swallowed down with a glass of tap water. Coffee was only second – the bitter brown with Snow White and the Seven Cubes gulped down to make me normal in appearance only.

I did not enjoy sucking or chewing on the precious toenails until later in the day. In an ideal world I would have ample supplies of toenails to swallow down like pills no matter what time it was. But some mornings I had to start by chewing. That was often the case these days. Toenail supplies were becoming shorter by the day.

Next to my bed, resting on the table, I kept an ashtray. It was meant to contain toenails but its usual state these past few months had been one of complete emptiness. Not even the dust of toenails was contained in it. A despairing sight, enough to send me plunging to the depths of clinical depression. Prozac could not cure my need for toenails.

I needed a full ashtray encase I woke in the night with a bad case of the nibbles. Cravings would keep deep sleep forever out of my reach. Prozac did not help in that matter either. In fact, I was beginning to believe Prozac was a pill of exceptional uselessness.

My wife's toenails were clipped away. I made her apply special paint three times a day to keep her in a state of permanent nail infection –they were stronger that way and hit my blood with more speed than an injection of diamorphine. But she needed toenails for it to actually work. My addiction kept them trimmed down to the cuticle.

The baby, I could chew on his toenails without clipping them. In fact, such behaviour was encouraged by the health visitor. Despite his regularly increasing sizes of clothing, his toenails did not grow quick enough to satisfy me.

It would be seen as cruel (and noticeable to that damn cock-sucking health visitor) to give my baby son a fungal nail infection but in the darkest hour, when the moon had set and the sun had yet to rise, I would sneak into the bedrooms of the other two and apply two coats of my wife's special paint. She was aware of what I was doing – powerless to stop it. Some credit is due my intense hen-pecking of her; she was too emotionally beaten down to protect her snotnose brats.

I was God's gift, or so I had managed to convince her. God's gift of what, she never enquired. Maybe God's gift of toenails? She would never be capable of surviving without me anyways. Submissive and emotionally beaten, that was how I liked her. The only love I had to spare was for toenails.

Sometimes, I wished for her to transform into a man. When I could not source enough toenails for satisfaction, dick cheese was an acceptable offering to the gods of withdrawal. I did not know whether, in the fundamentals of sex change operations, female-to-male transition resulted in the cheese of the gods though. If I snapped my fingers, she would go through with it to please me.

My ashtray was empty. Not even the ghosts of toenails lingered. It was a state I did not much appreciate waking up to. Before shaking could take over, I ran a finger into my foreskin – dry, always so fucking dry.

My wife snored next to me, oblivious to my predicament in the warm arms of her dreams. Sleep was the only escape she had. I was kind enough to allow it provided she kept her feet wrapped in the socks I supplied her with twice a year.

I told her last night that we needed to raid the graveyard behind our house. After a dull day at the office, energy was sucked out of me and I did not have the strength. But she could have done it on her own accord. As long as it served me, I had no objections to her doing stuff. Had she woke me up to a full ashtray, I may have woken her up with my cock in her throat as a reward.

It was the semi-fresh corpses that held the best toenails. I was sure to describe this to her in detail. On this occasion, she refused to take my hints and point-blankly told me that she would not aide me. I did not want her to aide me; I wanted her to go out on her own and dig up bodies.

'There was no babysitter' she cried, ignoring my hints about my total lack of energy. It was true, but the little snot nose brats would be okay for a few hours while they slept if I had the strength to join her and point in the direction of the fleshiest corpses with worms squirming out of their ears. They would never even know they were left alone in the dark. Prior to her recent maternity leave, I left them every night she was out of town on her intense, work-enforced training programmes. I did not like this recent boldness she was displaying. The health visitors fault entirely for encouraging her to attend Mum and Baby groups at the local library. And I would not be going! I did not know what part of my hints and manipulation she failed to understand.

The shakes hit me before I even switched the alarm to the snooze function. Withdrawal would not allow me the pleasures a snooze offered. It has not done for many years now. There was a time when toenails were plentiful and I could swallow one down while pressing the button for eight more minutes of blissful sleep.

Clamminess washed over me. There was no way I would be able to make it to work like this. I needed toenails to start my morning right. In the grips of withdrawal I could not think of anything other than toenails and scoring toenails. Toenails were all that mattered.

Ripping the duvet away from the wife was the difficult part. She held it in death's grip beneath her chin and tucked between her legs. I became used to never having any blanket – not even a little patch. I would crank up the heat when I woke with my midnight toenail cravings regardless of the season; a little bit of spite courtesy of good ol' dad. My wife would still be reluctant to liberate the duvet despite sleeping in a pool of her own sweat that turned the flakes of dead skin into slush. I once tried to satisfy my cravings with this skin slush; day-long diarrhoea left me on the toilet and the family had to use the outdoor one.

Shaking, it was more difficult to pry the duvet away from her. The withdrawals became worse each day. It seemed her grip on the duvet became tighter as the withdrawals became worse – her subconscious conspiring against me. The back of her mind knew I was no good for her and should trade her in for a younger model.

I only needed access to her feet. Toe jam wasn't as good a substitute for toenails as dick cheese but I needed to make it into work today and every other day for the rest of the fucking year. The board of directors were the biggest bunch of loser arse-ferrets this world has ever seen. I could not even provide an accurate description of what it was I did all day or a clear title for the job that would be on the line if I had a sick day.

TWO

I slid off the bed to the barren floorboards and pulled myself along. It was a ritual I repeated every morning as of late. If my wife wasn't so fucking stupid she would have understood my hints and filled my ashtray while I was gripped in a nightmare world where people were born without toes.

She was forced to sleep wearing microfiber socks and her wet feet coated in Vaseline every night to lock the moisture in. It was the best I could do given my limited resources and inability to think until toenails flowed like a waterfall. Even just a little lick between the toes would starve off the shakes long enough to break into the neighbour's bedroom with my nail clippers. There must be some way I can induce my penis to produce dick cheese for these early morning wake up calls.

The world pressed in. Everything tried to stop me from reaching the toe jam. Even the little splinters on the barren floorboards conspired against me and my addiction. Her feet; so far away they might as well have been located in Lapland dancing with Santa's reindeer. The situation lacked any hope of fulfilment, yet I pulled myself along the floor, taking splinters to my stomach when my silk pyjama top rode up and the matching bottoms rode down.

Dani Brown

The stupid bitch I married failed to notice my weight loss (toenails were becoming scarce; I could not eat a normal meal without first nibbling on a toenail or three). She should have noticed and purchased me new pyjamas weeks ago. It only made my hate for her stronger. Hate and resentment were two emotions to make it through the shaking cloud of withdrawal. They came out stronger on the other side.

She farted; a smell that could gas us both, somehow escaping through the fifteen TOG duvet, descended upon me like a million annoying nit-picking scorpions intent on stinging me to death but lacking enough venom to do it. My progress seemed lost in the gas but that was all in my head, the result of the withdrawal I woke up with (it became more intense every day).

I pulled myself along by the forearms – my pyjama bottoms found home around my ankles. Shaking them free would require a different sort of movement, one I could not muster the energy to do while hugged tight in the chocking grip of withdrawal.

If it weren't for the toxic gas leaking from her anus, I would be able to smell the toe jam. Just a few more pulls and I'll have my lips wrapped around her big toe, tonguing between them and licking all the sour goodness. The smell of her feet would keep my motivation high. The chances of her toxic arse gas evaporating were slim to none – there was nowhere for it to go.

TOENAILS

My thoughts were not coming in clear – a consequence of inhaling her toxic arse gas and not my own withdrawal. I could always think of toenails and toe jam with utmost clarity when in the grip of withdrawal. Anything to do with toes while in the heights of withdrawal would bring enough comfort and clear thought to score my next hit. But not while my wife's arse was leaking.

Dick cheese spread on toast had a similar impact but not the same as toenails. It was something I had to purchase from drug users in dark alleys. Work has kept me late for the past month, meaning I missed the junkies each night on the way home.

Toxic arse gas was something my body never built up resistance to. Twenty plus years of marriage and I still could not figure out what made her fart and subsequently ban her consumption of it. A blizzard of dust and splinters blew into my face, kicked up by her gas. Withdrawal made my eyes stick out – it would be impossible to close my lids against the assault.

The pain would be there until I wrapped my lips around her toes and sucked away the toe jam and mould lurking there. It hurt to breathe. Each inhale past my shaking lungs was like bringing in microscopic glass shards into my body – tiny sharp edges made me bleed. It was all part of the morning ritual.

Dani Brown

Low to the floor, one would be lead to believe I would remain unaffected by her toxic arse gas. The concept was all lies! Once it rose and had no more ceiling to press against, it would have to fill up other spaces in the room. I knew double glazing was a bad idea. The windows sealed the box that was my house and made it airtight to save energy. I was taken in by the sales rep and the pitch she gave as I imagined her on her knees sucking me off immediately following a complete toenail extraction.

Just another six inches and I could pull myself back onto the bed and taste my wife's festering feet. One more pull of my body lagging behind my forearms (limp and dead weight – shaking made it more so) should do it. Breathlessness overcame me by the time I was there. At least less toxic arse gas entered my lungs.

To rest would mean to allow myself to be overcome by the shakes. I needed a nibble before the vomiting and explosive diarrhoea hit. One nibble was all the preventive medicine my body required.

I had been here many times before – every single morning for the past two months, since toenails had started to become scarce. I could not take it much longer. There was no logical reason to explain the recent toenail scarcity. They simply were not growing as fast as they used to, yet my craving remained the same.

I pulled myself back to the bed. Her feet weren't wrapped in the duvet. Their odour could not overpower the scent of her farts. There was not a smell known to man capable of doing that.

The first sock seemed stuck, as it did every morning. They were hard to grasp with the shakes. By the time I had my tongue between her toes, I would forget my intention to buy her Velcro to sew to her crusty socks and myself a pair of gloves with Velcro sewn to the finger tips. Pulling them off would become easier – provided her foot bacteria did not cling on too tight. Walking past Velcro in the supermarket would not remind me of my intentions as long as I had a recent hit of toenails. It was not likely I would go into one of those places without one – the bright overhead lights and crying children hurt my head.

My wife was forbidden to bathe her feet. Mould would grow over night to satisfy my cravings in the morning. I wished for her toenails to grow as fast. No matter how many tablets I ordered online promising rapid nail growth and forced her to swallow, they never seemed to grow quickly enough.

I chanced a nibble. Flesh beneath the mould greeted my teeth. There weren't even cuticles to eat. Toe jam would keep me going through the morning. It would have to. The need to source a fresh supply of toenails was strong. I must sort it out tonight while the world lay in dreamland.

THREE

The day was long and hard. Working conditions were becoming worse as wages went down. Toenails being in short supply did not help matters. Any chance of job stability was ripped away by the board of directors during the summer when the entire office was forced into redundancy and rehired on temporary contracts.

Towards lunchtime I found myself crawling along the floor in the toilet searching for toenails. There were lots of dust bunnies but nothing resembling toenails – I took that to mean Health and Safety allowed the cleaners to sweep dirt into a corner but not to run the mop along the floor afterwards.

Everyone wore shoes to work. If damn hippies were employed, Health and Safety regulations dictated they kept their toes covered (it was a fucking office; there was nothing there attacking toes), which was unfortunate for me due to damn hippies having preference for bare feet or open-toed sandals. A secret bucket list item of mine was a trip to the Burning Man festival. Health and Safety regulations made no sense. It was a fucking office. Unless a computer spontaneously decided to jump off a desk and onto someone's foot, toes would not be broken.

During my lunch break, I went to visit a dominatrix. Mistress let me nibble her toenails for a hefty

TOENAILS

fee and beat me with a stick when I became carried away (she charged extra to my credit card for the beating). As I had already sampled her toenails, curbing the withdrawals, the beating felt good. She did not do it every day. Every time she did, the instrument changed.

My wife knew of my trips to the lunchtime dominatrix – the welt marks covering my body made it obvious. Due to my wife being a stupid bitch, I did take a few minutes to explain. I wanted to demonstrate only the stupid bitch wouldn't hit me. It was then I started to realise I had married a frustrating cow. She wasn't always that way. Years of my toenail addiction put her firmly under my thumb in areas she could comprehend. Her spirit died long ago.

My lunchtime dominatrix kept me going through the second part of the work day. If it weren't for her I would have been sent to rehab. Rehab doctors and nurses would not believe my addiction was to toenails. They would not be capable of taking in what I said and understanding the negative results of my drug tests. I would leave addicted to methadone and the users in recovery would be left without toenails.

As the minutes ticked by I found my concentration waning and my thoughts returning to toenails. Mistress needed to find me another dominatrix or escort with unclipped toenails. My request would make her jealous and I would get an extra beating. In the end, she would see the sense of it and call over one of her friends.

I asked a co-worker to cut his toenails and wrap them in cling film. He believed my story about needing them to put a hex on upper management. They did not last long despite how curved and yellow they were.

At this rate I would be shaking too badly for a late night trip to the cemetery. Everyone was too busy to pay heed to my pleas. If they did not have a family or a cat to return home to, there were bottles of whisky and vodka at the off license waiting for them. It took precious minutes to go into the toilets and cut toenails, which would mean more minutes spent in the hateful office doing a job they did not have the words to describe (because the words didn't exist).

FOUR

The multi-story car park was a desolate place. Half the lights did not function at all. At least half the ones left flickered in a photosensitive epileptic's idea of Hell. I never knew them to be efficient. I had worked there for years. Never had the carpark been a happy place. Whoever owned the crumbling office tower owned the carpark too. The lights added to the over-all depression. The slits in the walls did not allow in much natural light (especially in the winter). They did, however, let in the cold and the damp.

There was a set amount of work I had to attend to before upper management would allow me to leave the office. They monitored everyone. Withdrawal symptoms ensured I was often late to leave. It was outright impossible to work with any efficiency without toenails. If they would just let me leave on time I could spend my nights sourcing toenails at the cemetery.

The stress of it all made my cravings stronger. They visited with increased frequency. It was impossible not to notice all the employees in states varying from 'stressed' to 'experiencing stress so extreme they were breaking from reality'. The board of directors were either the biggest fucking morons on the planet or so sadistic and evil their intentions were to drive their workforce to suicide. Then there was the sheer pointlessness of it all.

My job had no purpose. Neither did that of anyone else who worked there. The company existed for the sake of existing. For those of us with addictions, it only served them. It was only a matter of time before the board brought in mandatory drug testing so they can sack everyone – except for me, toenails don't test positive for anything.

Clutched in withdrawal's shaking embrace, I still was not allowed the luxury of leaving early to feed my (non-chemical) addiction. Lunchbreaks were under threat. If they go, there's no way I'll be able to cope without my lunchtime dominatrix. Breaks were mandatory by law but the government turned a blind-eye to companies that broke them – something about strivers versus skivers.

Upper management were forced to stay late too by the board of directors. No one was spared the evil scumbag treatment. The lot of us were disposable. The overall goal, apart from increased productivity, was to drive the drones to their death. The world was overpopulated. The board of directors get rich/stay rich; we stay poor while our minds race around in circles chasing toenails.

The two stepping out of the elevator were from my office – part of upper management. Their frames were tiny; starved– even their bloated salaries were not enough for adequate nutrition (or they spent all the money on cocaine). Their hair; dull and listless. Skinniness did not impact upon the quality of toenails unless the person was compensating for their eating disorder by smoking crack.

In the flickering gloom they would not have seen me, although my teeth grinding echoed off the walls and travelled around, creating the perfect soundtrack to murder. The sound could be mistaken for the multi-storey carpark creaking with premonitions of collapse. It had been known to do that, yet no one came to fix it or close it down.

The women chatted without humour. It seemed they were in the midst of a conversation about over-throwing the board of directors. Munity was a great idea if they could accomplish it. They would need to round up all the employees and while they were over-throwing one office, they might as well over-throw the entire building, with staff joining from everywhere until the government were paraded and hung.

My craving was too strong to find out if they were serious. When the need for toenails took hold, I could not do much to contain it. I stepped out of the shadows and bashed the blonde over the head with my battered briefcase (all it contained was old batteries and my travel pedicure kit). I carried it around to feel special. I may have knocked out the only hope for office workers up and down the country.

Her friend was stunned into silence. Heels echoed off concrete as she backed away. I had to hit her too before she went for help and arrived back with the bobby on the beat. Chances of him (or her) knowing his (or her) own name was slim to none but that would not stop an arrest being made for assault. There wouldn't be toenails in a holding cell.

She was too shocked to fight back and went down like a puppy. My nocturnal excursions kept my body nice and fit. Even gripped tight in withdrawal I could knock someone (two someones in fact) out. I couldn't admire my work. I needed to taste the toenails between my teeth before any feelings of accomplishment and achievement could blind me to my addiction.

Tights rank pretty high up on the list of things I despise. They are so difficult to remove I've forbidden my wife from wearing them. I could not forbid them from being sold, although I did shoplift them whenever I had the opportunity. It was a little challenge I gave myself. I liked seeing if I could beat my record.

They were a tease; I could see the toenails lurking just beneath but could not taste. Toenails wrapped in fabric did nothing to satisfy the gods of withdrawal. Normal fabric I could deal with unless in the grip of particularly violent, withdrawal induced delusional shakes. These thin nylon, nylon/silk blends and one hundred denier wool blends were so fiddly. Shaking fingers couldn't grasp it.

Tights were like an extra layer of trousers beneath the skirts. Leggings I did not mind due to the toes being open. But tights were something else entirely.

I wished I could travel back in time and kill whoever invented them. It would be a slow and painful death for all the hassle tights have caused me over the years. People are buried in them, even if the deceased is dressed in a wedding gown with a twenty foot train. What is the point? No one sees the legs.

Necrophiles weren't fond of tights either. They could not work out why someone would go through all the effort of pulling the things onto a corpse. I sympathised with them to an extent but it was worse for me – no one had withdrawal symptoms from not sticking their dick in a gooey tight spot with worms leaking out.

These women were only knocked out. Removing tights in such circumstances was more nerve destroying than taking them from a corpse. A dead person couldn't wake up at any moment during the process demanding to know what was going on.

The women would think they were about to be raped. That was an honour reserved just for my wife. With the threat of forced sex looming over them, I would be attached. Withdrawal would not stand for that. The police will come along and find me cowering in the corner of the multi-story carpark ripping out what remains of my hair.

FIVE

Dead women would be better women. The need for toenails consumed me. It isn't like I had a decent set of morals to begin with; making the jump from beating people up and grave desecration wasn't a big one to make.

My body trembled. Murder would mean I would never overcome my addiction. The line was draw. My need for toenails did not care I was about to step over it. The trembling was the last of my morals leaving, pushed out by the shaking of withdrawal. Morals did not linger like a ghost. With that cleared up, I required a weapon before I lost sight of myself in a sea of withdrawal and had to plead for my cellmate's toenails.

Tights would be ideal to strangle someone with but if they weren't so fiddley the women would not need to die – I would clip their toenails and be out of there long before they could wake up. The women's choice in hosiery determined the course of my evening. I was okay with that. More than okay.

My shaking hands reached for my tie. The knot was a fiddley device I dealt with five days a week, twice a day for many years now. Withdrawal could handle it; it handled it every other week day of my adult life without many issues. Taking it off was easier than putting it on.

The problem, I only had one tie – there were two women (and twenty toes). Both needed to die. Death did not need to be long and drawn out. It would delay my access to toenails if it was. I could be creative later once I had toenails coursing through my blood stream.

Withdrawal prevented further contemplation. It prevented a lot of things. It encouraged murder. Murder could be viewed as a good thing – eliminating some scum on an overpopulated planet lacking in the resources to feed and clothe everyone.

Unconscious, the women could not put up a fight. Something tight around their necks could wake them. The worst possible outcome was the one being strangled waking and then in turn waking the other one, allowing her to escape. That would leave me without toenails and answering police questions while suffering through withdrawals.

Nights spent exhuming graves gave me a lot of physical strength when my body was not wrecked by withdrawal. I could have snapped her neck without the tie. I would have thought of that first if it weren't for my need to have toenails then and there. It clouded my thoughts rendering me slow complete with the occasional drip of drool out of the corner of my mouth.

Murder was a learning curve on the way to become a serial killer. Once the line was crossed, I felt empowered. Killing was easier than digging up graves. I

TOENAILS

had a wife that could go get my midnight supplies of
toenails while I slept like a baby.

SIX

Bodies take a while to cool and become rigid. In theory, it made my task easier. Or, it would have, if it weren't for the shakes. The rapid twitches made everything more difficult. Trying to take a piss while in the heights of withdrawal resulted in urine spraying everywhere. No one at work would use the toilet after I had been for fear of slipping and falling.

Burning liquid leaked out of my arse – much like a heroin user, withdrawal stage two involved stomach cramps and diarrhoea. The physical requirement to plug the flow; to taste those toenails between my teeth and allow them to graze my tongue to solidify everything before my arsehole exploded. Diarrhoea tablets had no impact on this type of diarrhoea. Nothing apart from toenails did.

My fear of the woman waking if I tore her tights became non-existent with her demise. Her death did not make removal of them any easier. It only removed the stress of the thought of her waking up and accusing me of sexual assault. Her words would lead to a holding cell undergoing more withdrawals due to my lack of access to toenails.

I tore into the tights creating ladders. A little piece of flimsy fabric could not have been hated so much. Even with the ladders, access to toenails was denied. More burning liquid leaked out of my arsehole and into my pants (if I don't get my teeth into those toenails, I will make my wife lick it).

The twitching movements fought for control. My body fought back. The toenails lurked just beneath the sheer fabric. My fingers worked it over, tearing it to pieces. The tights did not need to be removed entirely – I just needed access to her toes.

Time moves at a slower speed during withdrawal. The risk of being caught made it slower still. The sight of toenails without the taste made it stop entirely.

The fabric had a tear near the ankle. I pushed my fingers into it. It was as close to the toenails as my ripping had reached. All I needed was one more ladder before I could wrap my mouth around a toe and bite down. With her being dead, I would not need to be careful. There might be something in cannibalism to stave off the withdrawals for that bit longer.

Running my finger down the inside of her tights took forever. Shaking moved my hand from side to side. It was no longer a little bit of seepage coming out of my arse. It became a waterfall – I knew a tidal wave was next. My stomach tied itself into knots. It was building.

The sound of the tights ripping was not as pleasurable as I thought it would be. In fact, it set my teeth on edge leading to grinding. My dentist is going to be outright gleeful when he realises how much he will get paid to repair the damage.

I was down to the last inch before I could taste the toenail goodness. The last was always the worst. More liquid stained my underpants as the shakes became worse. Shaking tore parts of the tights that did not need to be ripped. It was senseless, torturous backtracking.

I grabbed my wrist with my other hand in an attempt to steady it. My entire body was shaking so there was not much point. It was the only thing I could think of to gain control. Concentration was added to it. If I could push all thoughts of physical withdrawal to the back of my mind for this last little inch I could have the precious toenails lurking beneath the tights.

Concentration was impossible with stage two withdrawals wrapping her fingers around my intestines and stomach. They weren't a stress ball, but trying telling that to her. She came with extra shakes too.

I pulled with all my strength before stage two gave way to stage three. Stage three was violent in its pain. I did not want to meet it – the toenails were in sight. Less than an inch now. There was a time not so long ago where I would have been able to taste them at this point before I put my tongue on the tips.

The fabric tearing sent some vomit up. It lacked toenails. I always wondered why my vomit lacked toenails, I certainly ate enough of them. If I could learn to regurgitate them it could stave off withdrawals in a pinch. I swallowed it back down knowing it would do me no physical good – I was so close to the toenails, I did not want to taint them with what I ate today mashed up and liquefied with stomach acid.

After what seemed like eternity, her tights were in tatters and the toenails were revealed. I did not pause to admire them. Stage three withdrawals were on the horizon, I couldn't stop with that threatening to paralyse me.

As soon as my teeth bit down stage two withdrew her fingers from my intestine and stomach taking the shakes with her. There was dirt beneath the nail. It was like receiving a prize in a box of imported cereal.

I bit into her flesh. I was curious to know if it tasted like pork or chicken (accounts weren't very clear and often disagreed). Cooked it might have been better. If there's time once I've gathered enough toenails to see me through the night, I'll saw off part of her thigh for my wife to cook for Sunday lunch.

Toenails tasted so good but I had the second woman to deal with now my craving was satisfied. The risk of her waking up was high. My briefcase over the head would not keep her out for long. In the grip of withdrawal, passing of time was a funny thing leaving me without a clue of how much had actually passed. If she were to wake, I would be discovered and she would call the police, thus destroying the chance of a decent night's sleep.

I took a chunk of toenail with my teeth to keep the withdrawals at bay while I went to work. There was no need to use my tie – my hands were strong enough after twice-weekly nocturnal grave digging these past few months.

SEVEN

Killing the second woman was easier. My lesson had been learned the first time around. I could save time and effort if I did it with my bare hands. I snapped the neck of the second woman – her name danced on the tip of my tongue but I could not recall what it was. My lack of memory would drive me crazy. I'm sure I'll be reminded at the funeral if it did not come to me by then.

I'm not sure if I'll enjoy having clear thought or not. The name, or my lack of memory of it, had the potential to drive me insane. Small details get missed when one is gripped in some stage of withdrawal. I needed more and more toenails to keep me going. If it weren't for the physical stages of withdrawal I may consider cutting down so I could always be on top of my game. First thing I would do is apply for a new job with a clear job description and some meaning. Alas, that would never happen for me – the need for toenails consumed me.

Lots of people were forced to stay late by the cunts on the board. The managers took it out on the staff beneath them. Leaving would be scattered. Taking in my surroundings in all their neglected multi-story glory made me realise there were a lot of cars left in the carpark. I either worked faster than I thought or those employed with me were really slow. This many cars would present the opportunity for a lot of fresh toenails.

If I could tame the symptoms of withdrawal and hide the bodies in a dark corner, I could bash people over the head as they left the elevator and keep myself in toenails all night long and maybe even until the next morning (my wife was being sent to the cemetery regardless of how many toenails I collected). I would save them for those three in the morning emergencies like a heroin user not yet at the full blown junkie stage.

I clipped the toenails and carefully put them in an apple seed bag with a hemp leaf printed on it. Residue of marijuana lurked in the far corners. When I found it on the pavement outside my house I thought "today is my lucky day". If only it was filled with toenails instead of a useless green plant. I rinsed the reefer out (except in the far corners where it clung tight) and left it to dry in the bathroom. It in no way would help my withdrawals.

Discovery of the little bag offered my wife a few hours of security – she confessed she thought I had switched drugs of choice and would grant her permission for a birthday pedicure when she goes in to have her fingernails done. How I laughed. It was hard enough to descend me into a fit of coughing. Instead of assisting me or getting me a drink of water my stupid wife backed away, not even picking up her feet until she was out of the room – only then did she feel confident enough to run. I heard her stampeding between my coughing. That night I cut her toenails down to the cuticle.

The following night she was forced to curb crawl until she brought me the most diseased looking prostitute of all. She filmed while I shoved my bare cock into the hooker and bit down on her toenails. Before the woman was sent on her way with double pay I fucked my wife. Blisters had already oozed pus down my cock. I viewed this as extra lubrication.

I smiled at the memories taking out the bag always brought. Good times.

It did not, however, help me move the two women to a place less likely to be seen by people stepping out of the elevator and into death's neck-snapping embrace. Dead bodies were rather heavy, especially when fresh with nerves twitching and bloated with gases yet to escape.

I did not expect them to twitch. The graveyard offered nothing as fresh as these two. Not even the funeral parlour had the twitchers. Had I not been chewing on a toenail I would have screamed before the cogs in my brain moved, digging out a memory of a documentary I once watched which explained what happened to the body after the heart ceased to beat and the lungs and bowels emptied.

The funeral parlour installed a sophisticated surveillance system last year. I have yet to figure out how to override it and replace the footage with hard core Mexican porn fresh from the farmyard. Robbing the funeral parlour was so much easy than digging up bodies once they were in the ground but murder might be the easiest solution to my addiction of them all.

Grave desecration was a full body workout but I was just after toenails. It seemed such a waste of time and effort. I left the bodies in their pine boxes for the necrophiles, aiding my fellow man in these times of austerity and all.

My night time digging did not prepare me for the weight of these two women (or the fucking twitching). I would rather have worms falling out of their cheeks than the gases building up. Of course the gases weren't actually building up after a few minutes (that shit could take days) but the addict's imagination is a funny thing, ripe with paranoia and easy to gross out. The flickering lights did not do much to help. I needed my next toenail fix.

In the end, I dragged the deceased to a darkened corner by their feet. It goes without saying that I was careful not to nick their precious little toenails. I had a little nibble, and then out came my pedicure kit. Trimmings went into my baggie with the other– bringing a smile to my face. All except one, I popped it into my mouth – a reward for a job well done.

People might find it strange to step out of the elevator and see two discarded pairs of decent high heels.

TOENAILS

I moved them to the corner as well – I can give them to Mistress next lunchtime. Additions to her collection; all clients keep their dominatrix rich in shoes.

EIGHT

It would be ill-advised to kill everyone who came out of the elevator. My leaving for the day was time stamped and time of death could be determined with accuracy down to the hour – or so the crime channel lead me to believe; it was probably more down to the minute. Suspicion would fall on me and my habits placed under the microscope. My toenail problem might be viewed as a bit weird by law enforcement.

It was then I decided to fuck the next one so that it looked like rape-murder or murder-rape (something dead would lack the ability to resist). It seemed I would join my fellow grave diggers in breaking the final taboo. My cock quivered. I may pick up some sort of necrophilia disease to pass onto my wife.

The elevator chimed into life. It was with nervous tension and not withdrawal that I popped another toenail into my mouth. The hairs covering my body stood up. Time slowed but not in the same way it did during withdrawal. With the bodies stowed in the darkest of corners I decided to have my way with the next person to step out of the lift before I forgot my brilliance. It would become my first act of necrophilia – fucking the person while still alive could give them opportunity to escape.

TOENAILS

Man, woman – what did it matter? As long as I did. The motive behind fucking a dead body was to disguise the motive behind the murders. The death count stood at two so far, both of the women were missing their toenails. Detectives may find it a bit odd.

Turns out, the sex of the victim did matter. He was huge, a real gorilla of a man, tinted orange in colour – some of that from the flickering lights but most of it looked like an accident with a bottle of fake tan. Shovelling grave dirt and lifting lids did not prepare me for steroid enhanced gym sessions.

My mind was made up. Once it was set on something I could not change it. I went for it. I lunged, hands poised to strangle. His height made his head impossible to reach, even from a crouching jump.

It felt like I had run and jumped at concrete. The impact recoiled through my body. I could have lost my bearings if I was not so stubborn and intent on having enough toenails to see me through the night. A person that large was likely to have very large toes with large nails attached.

Blood dripped down the cut. It was the confirmation my mind needed that I had, in fact, hit a person and not a walking blob of concrete controlled by electronics and engineered to vaguely resemble a man. Without withdrawal strangling my mind the possibilities of robot employees were endless. Robots could bleed –

motor oil, under these lighting conditions, would resemble blood. I licked for a taste. Copper engulfed the taste buds touching the cut. It was the last bit of confirmation required.

He swatted at the cut and trail of my drying saliva as if it were nothing more than a fly. He looked from his palm to me and back again. A combination of understanding and disgust dawned on his face. He was engulfed in a state of shock; that a man as small, disgusting and hamster-looking as me would have the nerve to assault him, a big brute with hours spent in the gym each evening after work and steroids on constant flow through his bloodstream.

Processing this through his head, with all the steroids vying for attention, resulted in a delay in his recovery from his state of shock and an opportunity for me. I jumped on his back. His neck was not as easy to snap as the malnourished females. I wished there was a mirror to watch his reflected facial expressions.

His reaction was delayed (either from all those steroids or simply a case of having never before been attacked) but eventually he decided it might be a good idea to attempt to fight me off. Under normal circumstances, someone of his size would have found it easy – he did not count on the toenails ruling my life and my sheer stubbornness. Both of them combined to give me enhanced strength. They could never match his size though.

Convinced we were only bruising each other I found my body wanting to hop down. My mind was saying "no" – to do so would equal certain death. I clung to his back; his sweat seeped through my clothing. Despite the infeasibility, I desired a shower at that very moment. There weren't any showers near here.

His toenails would be extra-satisfying due to the struggle to get them. I wouldn't let go with their imagined taste on my tongue. All his sweat would be like adding salt. It occurred to me that it may set off a new level to my addiction. I didn't care.

I dug my nails into his scalpel. More dandruff than anything ended up beneath them, coming close to forcing the nails up. My jagged edges (attempts at feeding my addiction by chewing on my fingernails) must have offered him relief from the itching. I didn't want to offer him anything except death and a quick post-mortem fuck.

I went lower. His neck was like a tree trunk-whacking a plank of wood over it would only serve to break the wood. My hands would do no good but they tried as if they had a mind of their own.

But everyone has their weakness. It was a matter of finding his before the elevator stopped at this level again. Discovery with this brute still walking would only serve to have me killed, or worse, the police informed.

He should have been the one I let get away. It was too late for should-haves and could-haves. The brute showed no signs of going down. He would succumb – if he didn't, I would be the one to die and I couldn't face depriving the world of me.

The only thing I could think of was to stick my finger in my mouth, lathering it with spit and sticking it in his ear in hopes all those steroids resulted in extreme sensitivity. At the most inappropriate of moments my cravings for toenails kicked in despite having just been fed. But both hands needed to be on him –I couldn't stick one in my pocket to pull out my baggie and then use both to open it and pop a toenail into my mouth. I would have to deal with the withdrawal until the brute was dead (or at least unconscious).

Shaking would not seem to be the best way to take down the beast. At least on the surface of things. By all accounts, withdrawals are typically viewed as a burden to the sufferer. Under the orange glow he looked like a jack-o-lantern painted even more orange with rage. I could see flakes of dandruff and smell the perfume of his week old sweat. This early random withdrawal brought with it heightened senses and the shakes.

My wet finger in his ear acted as a conductor to the shakes and the centre of his brain. He was sensitive to it; I considered myself very lucky. He dropped to his knees. It was easy to break his neck after that. It took both hands and a chokehold to get past his muscles though. I was tired – the thought of increased toenail supplies kept me going.

NINE

I did not consider how I would move him to the dark corner until after I sucked on his toes. One brief introduction to Heaven before I returned to Hell (and pulled muscles). He somehow had the uber-rare dirt under his toenails. I was getting really lucky with nail dirt. My co-workers and people in the other offices had filthy toenails, something I could only consider to be a blessing.

It would be best to violate his body in the corner; if someone were to walk across the car park at that time, there'd be little chance of discovery. Removing his toe from my mouth was more difficulty, psychologically, than killing him. I clipped his toenails so I would have a snack while dragging him.

The two women were heavy; this guy was triple their size but I was never one to think things through – consequences could be dealt with later. Now that it *was* later, I wasn't sure I wanted to deal with it. If I wanted to escape the night without being arrested and chucked into a cell lacking in toenails I would have to move him.

My wife will be rubbing my back when I get home and I might have to give the graveyard a miss. I'd planned on that anyways; she could go dig up graves while I sleep peacefully for the first time in years. I wished she was here now. I would have her move the body by herself and film me while I violate it – I wouldn't be the world's first necrophilia porn star but it was a niche that was sure to earn a lot of money.

Dragging dead weight on such a brute of a man by his arms put a lot of pressure on my back – I had to bend over. The pavement in the multi-storey carpark was hardly what one would consider to be smooth. Someone should see to that. I imagine a lot of people are killed in carparks, or at the very least go missing. Carpark owners could have a bunch of serial killers and serial kidnappers suing them for personal injury and loss earnings for the time off work.

I tried his legs instead. Missing his shoes, I had to be careful not to nick a toenail. Bent over, I was not sure if I would stand straight ever again despite forking out a small fortune for my wife to have classes in the art of giving a decent massage. The pain could be overruled by the thought of toenails and popping one in my mouth for a spot of nibbling.

Between the elevator and the darkened body-stashing corner, miles seemed to appear. Obstacles stood between me and my destination. Oil spills became sulphuric acid lakes. Glass became impossible mountains. It all needed to be navigated around, lest I get a shard in my dick when it comes to violating the corpse.

My wife was going to have a tough time working all the knots and kinks out of my muscles. When she's done, she gets to make a visit to the graveyard. She can experience miserable agony for once in her sheltered existence.

The dark corner was not far, just the other side of the elevator. Without dragging a corpse behind me it would be ten footsteps. Ten easy footsteps for a normal person; a mile if hugged in withdrawal's sticky embrace.

My groans echoed off the walls, dark with the fumes of diesel. Heightened senses of agony turned to watching the pollution eat into the sounds of far too much physical effort.

Drag and pull. One foot behind the other. Repeat. I paused to pop another toenail in mouth. The protein taste came away in my mouth for delusion bliss. For a few vital seconds I lost myself in the task of what I was doing and nearly tripped over the leg of one of the girls.

TOENAILS

TEN

I needed to rest and gnaw on toenails before I could even think about getting it up. The physical exhaustion caught up to my body, cancelling the pumping adrenaline. I collapsed on top of a corpse ripe for violating. I needed a minute or five to give myself a rest.

The elevator opened and two people left, chatting. Their voices indicated one male, one female. I focused on them as my body adjusted to not dragging the corpse of a bodybuilder across a multi-storey carpark.

Their silhouettes betrayed their lack of steroid addiction and hours spent at the gym. Flickering lights gave them a dozen different shadows. These would be the ones I allowed to get away. They can return home tonight to their families – they may not be so lucky tomorrow.

My sense of instant gratification, honed by years of toenail chewing, was now being taunted by a lack of instant toenails and would surely be the death of me. Those two would have been much easier to take out than the bodybuilder despite there being two of them – the two women had been easy enough and they were my first kill. I'd learned since then. I was familiar with my own strength and neck snapping abilities.

The two just off the elevator were loud enough with their incandescent chit-chat that they did not hear my heavy breathing or my muscles popping back into place (although this latter was probably only heard inside my head). Laughter from the female shot straight through me. Any hope of having an erection could not be realised until after she left. Just as well; the flickering lights would cast shadows of me riding a corpse across the carpark – an unusual sight someone might want to investigate.

These two took forever. They would have all day to flirt tomorrow, locked away in the office out of my sight and range of hearing (they weren't from my office – or at least, I did not recognise them). And time for a quickie during lunch; everyone enjoys a lunchtime quickie in the supply cupboard.

If they did not get a move on, I would not have enough toenails to see me through the night. On a positive note, I had enough time to catch my breath and feed my addiction. If I kept feeding it like this though, I would run out of people to kill before I had enough. Boredom and annoyance could lead to excessive toenail consumption.

Toenails were the only thing I thought about long term (or at least for twelve hour blocks, which was as long term as I could get). No matter what and how many toenails I harvest, tomorrow I will find myself visiting a lunchtime dominatrix, followed by barely making it through the day due to withdrawal. The evening will see me murdering more of my colleagues and employees of the other offices in the building.

TOENAILS

I would need to change my habits; maybe even park in a multi-storey carpark attached to another office, or worse, a public one at some point. It would serve to keep the police off my back and provide fresh toenails. That level of planning made me nervous which led to increased toenail consumption.

I wanted to make it home with at least half a baggie of toenails. At this point, I was eating them within a few minutes of harvest. One night's restful sleep was all I was asking for. It wasn't so much. I knew of people who asked for more and their wishes were granted – I wasn't that different. All I needed was for the Gods of Toenail Clippings to bless me with some patience and will-power.

Patience to emotionally deal with the chit-chat and high pitch squeals of the two walking across the carpark and will-power to not need to consume as many toenails while I wait. I would wait for them tomorrow no matter how many hours had passed since tasting a toenail on my tongue. These two would not be so lucky to escape tomorrow's toenail gathering. I'll be sure to jiz in her glossy locks as well – an added piece of indignity on behalf of the suffering of my ears.

My addiction demanded more and more of me and toenails were becoming scarce. I would make sure that lunchtime tomorrow produced extra toenails. Vagrants were known to gather together, sipping from cheap bottles of wine in the park. I could take a detour from Mistress' dungeon on my way back to the office tomorrow. If there were too many people around for a kill, I could buy their toenails from them. I could probably even purchase entire toes off the ones with track marks.

Sometime during the female's high pitch fit of giggles and pig-like laughter, keys found locks. They came in separate cars – they both had spouses waiting at home despite the peck on the cheek he gave her in the gloom. That alone was worthy of death. It was my reckoning toenails tasted better from the feet of people living in sin. The worse the sin, the better the toenails.

ELEVEN

They drove off. Her car was worth a lot more than his. As I watched them go, making sure they did not see me, I wondered if he felt like someone had twisted his balls until they came a bit loose.

To get myself hard (as corpses just didn't do it for me) I looked at pictures of toenails curling over flip-flops on a beach – my idea of decent porn. The first twinges of blood hit my cock. At this crucial stage was when I needed to taste feet.

His feet were swollen with steroid use. The marks where the shoes had been tied and the fuzzy inside of his socks were indented into his dead flesh. It would remain that way forever more (or at least until it decayed and was eaten by worms). I felt the roughness of it against my tongue. The taste of the stiffening flesh was like the taste of anyone else's foot skin; familiar, yet unique. Each person had a subtle difference to their taste dependent upon a lot of things: natural variants for a start, foot creams, sock brand, laundry detergent. It all impacted upon taste.

His body hadn't even begun to cool. It wouldn't be like fucking something alive though. Alive, he would be able to squirm beneath me if he was a man of smaller size. Dead, he would lay there and take it as his ghost watched on, powerless. As long as there were feet involved it did not matter to me. The police would have attention focused on local necrophilia enthusiasts – those were the important things.

I needed to chew his toes to have a full blown erection. Toenails were the only thing that did it for me. I couldn't violate a corpse with ol' half-floppy. Pictures only helped me arrive to the stage where I might be able to get it up if there are toenails involved.

My last child was conceived via a cup, turkey baster and sandal catalogue with toenail clippings gathered from the local mortuary (before the CCTV was installed). To conceive naturally would have involved fucking my wife when that was what she wanted. I resented giving her what she wanted, even when it was what I wanted too. If it weren't for the vital extra ingredient of toenail clippings I would have no third child.

Bodybuilders have great feet. His were made better by his obvious injection points making the veins stick out. In life, if I wasn't scared and a bit bigger myself, I would have offered a foot rub. It would have been done with my tongue followed by cutting his toenails with my teeth. Something I would have been able to do before addiction turned me into a quivering shaking mess.

Strong and muscular, yet bodybuilders often neglect their feet – especially while in the shower (that next steroid injection is far more important). He paid enough attention to them for use as an injection point. The latest one had the hallmarks of an infection taking hold. Like other bodybuilders, bathing his feet was beneath him.

Unfortunately for me, the brute neglected the rest of his personal hygiene (dick cheese was good but only on toast). Beneath the laundered and pressed suit complete with novelty tie lurked under-garments stained with at least two weeks of sweat – the smell disguised by cheap antiperspirant body spray (on offer at the local supermarket; three for £5). I'm not a big fan of body sprays; I find that too much of them can render me disorientated.

His toes were so nasty my cock throbbed, threatening imminent explosion. His feet could have swooped out of the sky to scoop up dinner from a field of fluffy bunnies. The bunnies would have never made it to his mouth – his feet would have eaten them themselves.

Any toenails left by the time I was done with him could be saved for special occasions. The Gods of Toenail Clippings had at least granted me that much will-power. I did not have a separate baggie to put them in. I'm sure I'll be able to tell which ones are his due to the fact they're misshapen and very long. He must have experienced more than a few procedures to remove ingrown nails in his life.

Lying on his washboard abs would present the best opportunity for violation. As long as my cock entered a hole and jiz seeped out of whatever hole it was, the police would put the pile of bodies down to an act of necrophilia. My true purpose needed to be kept hidden from them. I could fool my colleagues into thinking I had a problem involving sunflower seeds but the police may want a closer look at my baggie. The connection would be made between that and the fact that these bodies all had their toenails recently clipped (it was obvious on the one with painted nails).

His underpants were in worse shape than his undershirt. That did not spell good news for me. Shit leaked through to the extent he should have considered incontinence pants. This was not normal, everyday sharting – even by the standards of a heavy steroid user.

Track marks made a game of connect the dots on his thighs. He was a heavier user than I thought. Without steroids he was probably the size of a stringy teenager. I assume that's how he found himself in bodybuilding. Being picked on for tininess, he found himself in the gym incapable of building muscle. A drug pusher took him under his wing and showed him the first steps of injection. It was easy to picture under the flickering lights.

Toilet paper clung to his arse hair. I could be grateful for that. It implied that when he made it to a toilet, he cared enough to wipe. But it was still rather gross. If my mind was not made up and urging me onwards I would violate the next person to step off the elevator. Stubbornness could be a rather frustrating thing.

When I return home to my wife I probably won't have a recognised sexually transmitted disease but I will have something – the light in the sea of shit. I intend on letting it fester in my body while I chew on toenails and she prepares our evening meal. Then before our children are even washed and in bed, I'll have her take it up the arse. There's a higher chance of an anal tear than vaginal tear and therefore a higher chance of infection. Punishment for failing to keep me in ample supplies of toenails.

I plunged my dick into the tight place, lubricated by his suspected irritable bowel disease and dying shit. The smell was the stuff snuff movies are made of (leaving me forever grateful they did not come in Smell-o-Vision). Breathing through my mouth was not much better. In my mind, the particles of shit were visible and I could see them dancing across my taste buds.

His toenails between my teeth brought me to ejaculation. My toes were shoved into his open mouth. I liked the way they hit against his teeth. My dick's odd shape and angle was not successful in fucking girls when I was younger. It seemed it had found its true purpose in violating a corpse.

TWELVE

Upon reflection, I could have sexually assaulted him with a stick. I always had more ease cumming with my hand anyways. Learning this new thing about myself did not make me want to fuck dead people any more than I had before. It was all about the toenails for me and always would be.

I had to clean myself before someone else stepped out of the elevator. I had already allowed two people to get away – everyone else could be my victims. If people would only donate their toenails to me without viewing it as odd, or worse, threatening to commit me to a lunatic asylum, I would not have to go through such drastic measures.

The frizzy mop of hair on top the blonde's head made for perfect cock-wiping. It also reinforced the idea that the killer's fetish was necrophilia and had nothing to do with feet or toenails. There were entire websites dedicated to hair cum-shots, so that was a fetish in itself. At the very least, I could make the killer look very confused. The local police forces were fucking morons anyways.

His toenails were impossible to cut. I could not spend all night in the carpark chewing on his feet. If I was not caught, I would freeze to death or choke on exhaust fumes due to the bad ventilation and boarded up vents (the various boards of directors had it in for their employees – probably had extensive life insurance policies on us all).

This man had toenails of such high quality that even if I was not addicted; I would not have been able to let them go. I looked around for quick inspiration (it had to be quick; the elevator could chime into life at any moment and stop at this floor with my next victim).

I had to disable the fire alarm for access to the axe. Chopping off his feet and bringing them home seemed like my best option. Two feet – prizes for my wife to put in deep freeze and serve up for Christmas lunch. She can pry the toenails off for me. If she damages them, she will receive the thrashing of her life.

I shoved the handle in and out of his legs to make it look like I had a thing for penetration of the dead. A pity really. My balls would build up enough time to at least get an erection by the time I arrived home to pass skin tears and diseases onto my wife.

THIRTEEN

The elevator chimed into life again as I knew it would. I'd already allowed two people to drive off; I was entitled to more toenails from office workers. I stowed the feet next to the bodies. I would have to remember to pick them up before driving home. Human flesh will be such a Christmas treat. I can't wait to see the look on my children's faces when I tell them what they had eaten for Christmas lunch (vomiting, of course, would be prohibited unless they intend on drinking it with a straw afterwards).

If I could get enough toenails to see me through the night, I will sleep the night through without nocturnal anxiety about withdrawal symptoms and the need to dig up graves to feed my addiction. Increased supplies of toenails would equate to sleeping better than I had done in years. The thought actually resulted in increased tension and anxiety. It could only be relieved by killing for toenails.

One lonely office worker left the elevator. I bashed her over the head with my briefcase. Killing was becoming natural for me and I had only been at it one day – I wished I had started sooner but it was too late for regrets now. She went down quickly; no struggle from that one, or maybe it just seemed that way after the brute.

TOENAILS

This one was cute. She did not smell bad either. It was such a shame to kill her. I was killing without first thinking things through. I'll need to break that habit if I'm to make a success out of this life and forever stay in supplies of toenails.

Her pretty fingernails were long, natural and unpainted. That was always a good sign. I knew that from excessive time spent digging up bodies and late night trips to the pre-CCTV morgue. I liked the taste of dirt beneath the toenails though. It was such a rarity that it was special.

I dragged her to my darkened corner. After lugging the brute the few feet from the elevator she was light, like picking up a small bag of flour from the shop. She smelled of soft perfume – it was gentle and welcoming, not overpowering. I wanted to eat her. Not in a cannibalistic sense, but indulge in a spot of muff-diving (something my wife never experienced from me, for all I knew she was getting it from the postman).

The first twinges of regret went through me. She was almost too perfect to kill. If my balls weren't shooting dust then I could have fucked her remains. If I couldn't have her, the necrophilia enthusiasts couldn't either. There were one million ways to disfigure a corpse, but first her toenails needed to be in my mouth and baggie.

Removal of her shoes informed me that she was not wearing any socks and probably hadn't done in a very long time. Perfection stared back at me in the form of blisters and toenails, filed but long with no paint. There wouldn't be any dirt underneath them, nor any sock fuzz. I hated sock fuzz – my wife's socks were all purchased by me to ensure it was kept to a minimum.

The pus from her fresh blisters was just delightful. The pus from the old blisters was even better. I had to work those ones over with my teeth, gnawing, but not enough to allow them to explode. I liked foot pus to ooze into my mouth allowing me to savour every drop.

There was no way I could bottle it up. I did not have anything to catch it in, except my mouth. As long as I was quiet about my slurping no one would notice me in the darkened corner. Even in adequate light, everyone was too over-worked, underpaid and totally demoralised to really pay much attention to their surroundings.

If I had known this woman did not like socks I would have kept her as a blister and toenail slave instead of adding her to the bodies in the darkened corner. A pile of bodies plus one kidnapping would confuse the police. If someone tiny steps out of the elevator I'll try to bare that in mind. Excitement about additional toenails may cause me to forget. Toenails were my life; blister pus was an added bonus.

As I did not know a thing about resuscitation and head injuries I went about cutting her toenails to add to my apple seed bag with the marijuana leaf printed on it. I popped one in my mouth to suck on. The taste was like no toenail I had ever had before. It needed savouring with a mouthful of pus. A moment to reflect on my plans for the evening and how refreshed I'll feel in the morning.

If my erection returned, I knew whose body I would violate. The chances were rather slim. I would have better luck shooting dust out of Ol' Mr Floppy all night. I was rather sad – addiction sucked my sex life out of me. Even when Mistress was working me, I could not get it up.

I looked around for something to remove her skin – the necrophiles did not like them skinless unless it was part of natural decay. I was not going to leave such a specimen of beauty for them to find. It was a secret club but a rather bigger one. At least five employees from the offices would have been in it.

I did not know the first thing about removing skin. In the end I scraped some away with the axe and tried to pull. It made a weird popping noise but did not come away with the ease I imagined. There was nothing to hunt in this country (except people). All our food came in packages from the supermarket, imported from God-knows-where. If hunting – real hunting, not that stupid shit with dogs on horseback - was popular I might have had a background in skinning and some vague idea of what I was doing.

As long as she was disfigured enough to stop Club Necrophilia jizzing in their pants then I supposed it did not matter. I hardly needed a human skin coat or lampshade. I did not have anyone to present such an item to. I did, however, have toenails to gather.

A razor blade would have been much more practical for skin removal and disfigurement. As it was, I only had the axe and nail clippers so I chopped off her ears. After doing the act, I realised it was like leaving a giant welcoming hole for the necrophiles. I plugged them up with the tights from my first victim. An observant necrophile would notice and pull them out to enter the hole of pleasure.

Her eyelids came away with ease. No one would want her with unless they could place pound coins on them to keep them shut (and pay her passage to the Underworld). I ate them; not as nice as toenails. Raw skin could not be chewed. But I had less of a chance of food poisoning than eating my wife's pork roast. In the end I had to spit them out like a piece of gum.

The elevator chimed into life. My work here would have to be done – there were more toenails to gather. With the speed of a fox scooping chickens from a coop, I clipped her toenails and added them to my baggie.

Energised, I went to stand by the elevator. This was the perfect way to give into my addiction. I don't know why I had not thought of it sooner. If toenails were social status, prior to this evening I had been firmly middle class. Now my need for toenails and their apparent abundance would force me into that awkward position

TOENAILS

the upper classes refer to as "new money" (in my case that might be "new toenails"). I didn't mind. If these folks weren't my co-workers, I could rob them as well and become actual "new money".

FOURTEEN

It was getting late. People would be revolting against the directors – not like any of us could describe what the company did or the purpose of their job. No one was capable of expressing their feelings of being fed up either. The best anyone there could hope for was someone waking up and starting a violent revolution. Nightly exodus and feelings of rebellion weren't enough to change the system.

I laid in wait. The elevator seemed to take longer even though it was not stopping at any other floors according to the electronic display above. The eyelids kept me satisfied. My body was enjoying the chemicals released with each new drug.

Hope grew in my heart for a silent one-by-one revolution in the office. I went through it every day the withdrawals hadn't claimed me. No one was that bright, it had been educated out of them, starting with children's television and emphasised at school to make the population compliant in marching towards their doom.

I swallowed down my hope with a toenail. It was a useless thing to feel. While there was still hope, nothing would ever be done. The more people that wake up the higher the chances that someone bright just might do something. I knew something needed to be done but toenails would not allow me to contemplate what.

Different people have different tolerances of bullshit. They caved into it each evening. They thought they were being so bad; the training and brainwashing had not grown deep roots in their brains. But they were wrong. The junkies knew something was wrong and eased with their substances.

These late nights and early mornings were wearing even the strongest down. It was easy to tell who had a drinking problem at the office. At least half the employees had whisky seeping out of their pores. I preferred my toenails. Not even a bottle of Jim Bean could dull those cravings.

The elevator sang its hymn of hope on my floor (the only hope I allowed myself) – another lone female stepped onto the reinforced concrete floor. Easy prey, or so I thought. If I'm going to do this every evening I need to learn to not judge. I could get killed that way.

This one had a few kick boxing classes and gave me a black eye before I managed to knock her out. She was strong, but not as strong as the brute (unless the eyelids had given me a sudden burst of strength and energy). I would experiment with more eyelids before I reach a conclusion.

I snapped her neck. The crack echoed off the dirty walls. Not many cars would be leaving this level of the carpark tonight if my suspicions about the eyelids were true. I had no way to preserve them. Tomorrow I will bring Tupperware and have a special homemade gum for the next day.

I needed another taste of the thick bitter goodness to see me through, courtesy of my pus queen with tights instead of ears. Death squeezed his way out to make way for the bloating gases. Pus was a wonderful thing. I had reached the conclusion that the taste of infection was much better than the taste of human flesh. What a perfect way to wash the blood away from my taste buds.

Blisters were a common complaint amongst women in the office – cheap high heels create painful sores. I would never run out. I could eat more eyelids to make me strong. And who knows, I might even grow to enjoy the taste.

Perfectly capable of cutting toenails with my eyes shut, I did just that with my tongue wrapped around the blister of one dead woman as I cut the toenails of another to add to my selection for the night. Withdrawal had left me. It may have been the addition of human flesh or the lack of anxiety about not having enough toenails – I have this feeling that it was really a bit of both.

My mood was as high as the clouds. The chance of a full night's sleep danced in my mind. I was excited for it – something I hadn't felt in such a long time it took a few minutes for the emotion to click and vague recollections of it to surface.

With the nails clipped and added to my baggie, I had time to lay in wait by the elevator. It was only my first night but I was really taking to my new role of killer. It was more doing my victims a favour – I scratch their back by putting them out of my misery and they scratch mine with their toenails (although it is more of a throat scratching). It was unfortunate I could not kill everyone on that first night.

Bodies piled up. The next few passed in a blur of toenails, human flesh and disfigurement. It was hard to say how much time had passed. The withdrawals had stopped entirely but my baggie became full as I was not consuming toenails as I cut them. It was time to think about heading home. Even if I don't force my wife into a middle of the night cemetery excursion I would have enough to last until morning.

The office was huge – the building it was in housed many offices of equal size. None of the offices had a set floor they could park on in the multi-storey carpark. That first night I met no one I spoke to on a regular basis. I'm not sure if that would have made a difference to my rampage or not.

My need for toenails would not make an impact on overall population numbers and each worker was disposable –it's not like our jobs mattered anyways. The pointlessness of our existence was what made killing so easy.

TOENAILS

FIFTEEN

The hour was late when I arrived home. The evening meal had already been served; mine sat on a cold plate on the counter with a plastic cover. If I was more interested in my family I might find myself rather pissed off about that but as it was, I preferred eating alone. The gravy had congealed – I had that as an excuse to be pissed off with my wife.

The snot nose brats were in bed, except the baby – that fucker never slept. I was much later than I intended. My cock had time to allow the bacteria to breed. My mood was too high for him to bring it down with his howling (or my wife and her congealed gravy).

My wife shot me a dark glance. I did not have a reason to care. I shot her back a look to make her cringe. Looking at myself under the bright glow of the shadeless overhead light I saw that I was splattered with blood and gore. She did not have the nerve to scream – I ruled the roost. She wouldn't dare.

I'm not sure if she noticed I was not shaking for the first time in what seemed like years. Catching glimpse of my reflection, there was a gleam in my eyes. Muscles used for smiling were being employed – it hurt but I could not help it.

Dani Brown

Before I sampled my congealed gravy I had a little leftover present for my wife on my cock. Squealing offspring can be left to roll around on a sheepskin rug with a pacifier shoved in their mouth. Not even the health visitor cares if a baby witnesses such acts of intimacy.

Bent over the sofa offered the best entry into my wife's virginal arsehole. One hand undid my trousers and allowed them to drop to my ankles; the other grabbed her by the hair. She knew what was coming. Her cries of pain and surprise sent quivers to my cock. It was actually filling up with blood. My balls still hurt a bit from the total drainage but it was a nice pain.

Unfortunately her cries woke up the other two brats (the health visitor would not like that). Her screams upon anal entry woke the neighbours – the volume of their television was sent right the fuck up, loud enough to rock the walls (on both sides). It was a tight fit. I would be hurt in this too but I did not mind. I wanted her to be laid up in bed sick, or desiring to be laid up in bed sick while she did the housework and brought the little brats to and from school with a high fever and chills.

The children came running downstairs to save their mother by slapping my arse at each thrust. It would not do them any good. Even if I wanted to pull away, I don't think I could – her arsehole was like a vacuum. The suction was intense. I might even reach ejaculation and make my little darling brats suck it out of her arse.

TOENAILS

Toenails were my thing; I left the kids fingernails alone. This translated to one of the snot nose brats that it would be okay to scratch me and make me bleed. They should have known better. I raised them better than that under the umbrella of fear. As soon as I'm done with their mother and certain she has the beginnings of a nasty bacterial infection I will punish it with broken wrists all around and a mouthful of my jiz mixed with their mother's shit and burning anal infection.

I needed toenails to cum. I pulled my wife down with me to reach into my pockets. I had a baggie full and it was overflowing. I knew I would be shooting more dust than semen – it wasn't important, as long as my snot nose brats had to clean it up, I wouldn't feel the pain. Emotional pleasure more than made up for it anyways.

There was no reason I could not break the wrists of one of the little snot nose brats now. I reached behind me as I pumped into my wife's arse, close to cumming for the second time today. Multi-tasking was typically associated with women; addicts were better at it – as whatever child I grabbed was about to discover.

The neighbours must have been getting an earful. If in nine months' time they have a new mouth to feed, I will send them a back dated bill for pay-per-scream porn. No one is allowed to get off on what I do without first being granted my permission and second, paying me (preferably in toenails).

Dani Brown

I caught someone by the wrist. I did not care which snot nose brat it was, as they would be on the receiving end of the same punishment anyway. Snapping a child's wrist was like scrunching paper into a ball only with the addition of screaming. The other one stopped hitting and scratching.

I kept my family obedient under an iron fist – even if the brats had enough intelligence to phone the police they wouldn't dare. This new-found rebellion was a temporary thing, egged on by their dreams of a world with normal parents.

I also read them bedtime stories printed from anti-government, anti-police, anti-military, and conspiracy theory websites to give them a healthy dose of paranoia in regards to authority figures and life in general. Both of them would cower somewhere until I was done (and cover their own buttholes with silver tape for fear of an anal probe – something to do with the noise attracting the attention of the greys). My wife was forced to put on a display of believing the conspiracy theories. She was a smart one once. I took such pleasure in breaking her down. That intelligence might linger in the back of her mind somewhere. Somewhere that knows the bullshit I spouted was all lies.

One of them had enough sense to pick up their little brother on the way to hide. I'm guessing the one without the broken wrist. I did not approve of this helping each other. Three of them together could overthrow my dictatorship while I'm gripped in withdrawal and delirious.

Now was the perfect time to confess murder to my wife. Details of my killing spree will serve as my children's bedtime story tomorrow. I'll make it extra graphic to scar them for life; not only is daddy a serial killer, he also told them all about it just before bed. I can picture the made-for-TV movie based on my story.

My wife had become bold lately – a consequence of those mother-and-baby groups the health visitor insisted she attend. It was still in her, buried somewhere. Taking out a feisty bitch and taming them was a badge of honour at university. More important than a degree was marriage to the biggest bra-burning, psychotic bitch of them all.

Telling her I didn't just kill one office worker but left a pile of them in a multi-story carpark to be gnawed on by rats will return her state back to extreme obedience and submissiveness. The feisty bitch inside will be buried once more. The best thing about this was that her intellect was actually greater than mine.

Her earning potential was much higher too. Forcing someone like her to live in misery was the best thing a man could do. All my old friends from university were jealous when I told them she knows when she is being manipulated but is powerless to do anything about it.

If my dick was not plugging her up, it was my belief she would have shit herself. She might have anyways. Blood and shit could be hard to tell apart beneath the energy saving equivalent of forty watts courtesy of the life-long supply the electric company sent out. A close inspection, post-ejaculation, would have been pointless.

She seemed especially squeamish when I told her I ate that woman's eyelids only to discover they were more like chewing gum and had to spit them out. Licking inside her ear forced her into coming pretty damn close to breaking her neck. I didn't want her to die; the children were too weak to dig up graves. I went gentle on her. I can always spit in her mouth when I force her into a night-time kiss with extra tongue.

She wasn't too impressed by my act of necrophilia either. I think it is safe to assume she thought I was strictly against it given how much time and effort I put into complaining about my fellow cemetery raiders. Her attempt to sink into the sofa would not spare her my cock.

It was being torn apart inside her. The brute bodybuilder had a loose arsehole in comparison. He either preferred the company of men, horses or big novelty dildos; I never thought to enquire about which. Still, he did give me a few cuts given how well I was hung.

TOENAILS

Mindful that she did not want me breathing into her ears, I turned my head away and made my final thrust for glory. Releasing into her, a howl escaped my throat. I made a note to bill the neighbour.

It was then I remembered the severed feet. Orgasm, especially when one does not reach it often enough, is like an explosion in the brain. Random thoughts appeared and died out as they went on to form the system that served as my thought process. I held onto the feet – a nice Christmas lunch for me and my family.

SIXTEEN

I left her to bleed and splutter. She would not have been capable of walking had I handed her the feet to put in deep freeze. I had to do it myself; better than them going to waste. My default non-withdrawal state of mildly pissed off kicked in. Mildly pissed off I might have been but I was not stupid; I knew giving them to her, the feet would not be a Christmas feast but instead fester for a week before being fed to the neighbour's dog.

Before going to search out my snot nose brats I pulled my wife's head back by the hair – time for a kiss. She clamped her jaw shut. Obviously she still had some disobedience left in her. I found it rather offensive. If I did not need her alive, both to raid the cemetery and embarrass, manipulate and control as a symbol of status in front of my friends I would have killed her there and then.

I pried her lips apart with my tongue and ran it along her front teeth. It was just what she needed in addition to a bedtime story about the taste of human flesh and the virtues of eating it. In the end, I had to squeeze her nostrils shut with my fingers to get her to accept my tongue into her mouth. She was too spent to run into the bathroom for mouthwash afterwards.

TOENAILS

In the middle of the night I would wake her and send her to dig up a grave from a funeral the day before to see me through until mid-morning break with enough toenails. An abundance of toenails would reduce my anxiety levels. I wanted a slice of thigh as well but the embalming chemicals could poison me – waiting for the next day sucked.

The snot nose brats lacked creativity when it came to picking a hiding spot. I found them in the cupboard under the stairs – the same place I always found them when they were frightened. The perfume of shit and piss greeted my nose. I knew it wasn't all from the baby. They can be punished for that as well. I did not appreciate the outward display of disobedience but the fear supplied wholesome nourishment and reason for additional punishment so I never put a stop to it.

If I could keep withdrawal symptoms at bay for long enough, I intended on setting up hidden motion activated speakers in there with a creepy industrial soundtrack playing at a volume just over the threshold of their hearing – just loud enough to further unnerve them. If I kept myself in toenails until the weekend, it will be my weekend project. I always did projects at the weekend – they were vital towards maintaining my mental health, even in the grips of withdrawal.

I pulled the intact snot nose brat out by the hair and shoved the other two away. The way the broken one held his wrist produced a Cheshire cat grin which must have made me look especially manic to my darling little snot nose brats. The broken one had already wet himself but that did not stop the patch growing as his bladder let go again (I must talk to my wife about allowing them a drink before bed).

Their mother was in too much pain to become involved. I could hear her sobbing howls from the next room. It seemed she was not capable of moving from the sofa even to rinse the taste of death out of her mouth. For once in our marriage she was bringing me happiness.

Visions of other families with the children tucked into bed while mum and dad sipped mulled wine and shared a secret kiss played across my head. My children would be spared the dullness and boredom of a childhood like the one I experienced. It would turn them into well balanced adults capable of coping with anything.

My daughter's wrist crumbled beneath my hand – never fuck with daddy. Daddy gave you life; daddy could take it away.

Medical treatment would be denied to these two unless their mother took them while I was at work, but she had problems of her own. She may not be able to get them there – incapable of walking due to anal damage. A raging infection will further immobilise her. An ambulance won't be sent for broken wrists.

TOENAILS

Everyone had a long night of pain ahead, except for me – not even my black eye hurt. I took out a toenail and popped it in my mouth, it was usually the opposite way around. I would suffer in agony all night long while the house slept soundly – except the fucking baby. I would look forward to hearing it but I was looking forward to a full night's sleep more. There would be time to hear the sounds of agony in the morning. It would be more intensive then as the pain would have settled in and took hold over night.

SEVENTEEN

A hot shower would rub the ache of murder out of my muscles. I was correct in my assumption. I did not want to brush my teeth or even allow water into my mouth though. The last of flesh and toenails lingered on.

This evening was my first real-life experience in the act of killing someone. It was more like an art. As much as I thought about it in the past, the opportunity to commit had never occurred before. It was my own fault really; we create our own opportunities and disadvantages in this life.

I was not worried about the police catching up with me. Even if they interviewed everyone employed in that particular office block I was confident I could outwit them. Short of taking a stool sample to prove I had consumed human flesh, there was no evidence.

The water rinsed all the blood away. I'll have my wife burn my clothes in the fireplace before the infection takes her. I helped myself to her shower gel; an expensive present from her sister. I wouldn't normally allow her such luxuries but her sister checked in frequently to make sure she used it and every other toiletry and bit of make-up purchased.

I was not one for bathing. My typical routine included a shower no more than twice a week. The scent and evidence of murder needed to be washed away. It may become a more common occurrence, perhaps even making me "likeable" to my colleagues. I would need to come up with a new people-repellent.

A warm fuzzy feeling engulfed me in the vapours and bubbles. I was in the mood for a mug of hot coco. I knew my wife kept some to calm the snot nose brats. I stepped out of the shower and ordered her to bring some up. The neighbours would have heard my demands. If she did not bring up some, they would – just for the simple fact that I would shout all night if I did not get any and they wanted to relax and sleep.

Despite her pain she would put in every effort towards obeying. I never left her with any other option. If my neighbours had to bring my hot chocolate, they might have to step over her. They never phoned the police or an ambulance – if they weren't so frightened of me I would conclude they were outlaws, paranoid about law enforcement and courtrooms locking them up.

If I wanted her to, she would get down on her knees and suck me off. So would the neighbour's wife. At a push the neighbour himself would to keep me quiet. He just wanted to get some sleep so he could be awake tomorrow for a busy day of getting drunk and watching daytime TV.

Saliva would not ease my friction burns and could possibly make them worse. Inspection of my cock revealed tiny skin grazes. I'm not sure if they occurred while inside the brute's arse or my wife's. I dried it on a clean towel and applied anti-septic (something I would not be applying to my wife's wounds).

If I was confident her spit would not result in blisters I would humiliate her further and stream the entire thing while the snot nose brats watch out of range of the camera. If I could be certain no pain would occur, I would go downstairs now and throat fuck her. There would be plenty of time for that tomorrow.

My wife's bathrobe was fluffier than mine so that's the one I wrapped myself in. I would not use her slippers though – I liked to keep my feet clean and fungus free with regular spa pedicures. Both were gifts from her sister, otherwise she would not have them.

I popped a toenail in my mouth. I wasn't shaking or even experiencing anything remotely resembling withdrawal. I wanted a toenail. I had abundance so I had a toenail. This simple act was something I had not been in a position to do for a very long time.

My children screamed and cried – a promising soundtrack of fear and pain to aide me falling asleep. They may even appear in my dreams, turning from nightmares into something pleasant. Never before had I felt so relaxed. Life was a constant stream of trying to find toenails and never having enough.

TOENAILS

My wife brought me up my hot chocolate. I took the opportunity to inform her she would not be sleeping that night. She did not seem surprised by the revelation. I did not expect her to. I ran my house under the threat of constant strain and expected completion of impossible tasks. If she did not do as I commanded and carry out a successful operation there would be consequences – none of them positive.

Nocturnal graveyard digging and caring for a screaming baby should weaken her immune system sufficiently to allow the anal infection to embrace her skin grazes and invade her blood stream. It would make cooking and caring for the house an outright impossibility but she would still have to do it. It'll bring me amusement watching her try as I grew fat on toenails.

She was resigned to obey. The feisty girl I married was long gone. I did not appreciate the health visitor trying to bring it out again. It took years of hard work and effort to get her this complying. Every whimsical demand I made would be met with little to no compliant.

I stirred a pinch of toenails into my hot chocolate. My wife should have pulled off the toenails of one of the little snot nose brats to put them in my drink but she didn't. I would punish the transgression tomorrow.

EIGHTEEN

I did not remember falling asleep. The alarm sounded. I was already entering the world of the waking. A full night's sleep meant I did not need something like an alarm. This was a new chapter in my life – one that would not be ripe with the misery of withdrawal.

My wife farted next to me. A sound that stuttered with shit, blood and the fresh pus of a new infection. I wanted to lick it. It would help me get through to lunch. Pus made the toenails stronger – like a cocaine addict cooking up crack.

I waited. I did not want to wake her. She might view that as trying to give her pleasure, or worse, actually loving her. I did not want either of those things. She was trapped and knew it. Nothing could change it except her frame of mind.

I was still in my wife's pink fluffy robe. I would bring it to work with me and leave it in the car. I did not like the thought of her being hugged by it. It may make her feel too comfortable and bring into the blissful unawares of sleep.

It was the first morning I woke up without withdrawal symptoms plaguing me for as long as I could remember. I watched my wife sleep, knowing she would be awake soon. The dirt from the cemetery toenails rested on my tongue. I might make it through the entire morning without any withdrawals. A positive attitude would see me through the day and make killing in the evening less physically draining.

My addiction spanned my entire life. It had grown worse in recent years. Keeping it satisfied was a task I was not up to. Until now. The discovery of the beauty of murder could keep me in toenails for the rest of my life. Carefulness was a necessity but I did not need to be that careful due to the stupidity of the local police officers. As long as I did not make any obvious mistakes, I could keep this up for years.

I popped another toenail in my mouth to keep any shakes at bay and examined my ashtray. My wife arrived home with a decent haul. My ashtray was nearing full. The necrophiles would have assisted; it was a club I could now claim membership of. But that did not explain the vast supply of toenails. There's no way she had that much help. The bedtime conspiracy theories plagued me with some slight paranoia – she was up to something. One last ray of hope to save herself and her children (which would always remind her of me, no matter what happened).

She farted her agreement. I knew it. The sound of sirens broke the frosty morning air, but it was in my imagination (and probably the dreams of my neighbour). Perhaps sending my wife to collect the toenails of the dead and buried was not such a good idea. Lesson learned. I could only hope it was not too late. There would not be an abundance of toenails in prison once I get through the feet of all the other prisoners and guards. Rationing them over the course of a life sentence would lead to my inevitable suicide.

My alarm did not wake the baby but my wife's toxic arse did. Before she could see to him I pulled off her underpants and started sucking her arse to wash the bad thoughts away. She tried to squirm away so I back-handed her. Unpleasant brain vibes needed to be washed down with anal pus.

The baby was her problem. Only after I sucked the pus out to wash down my toenails though. She would produce more during the day. She already felt hot and feverish beneath my hands and tongue.

The baby's screams would wake up the other children and my neighbours but I didn't care. My wife wanted to soothe him – I needed her arse pus. Once she realises where she is and the dreams of a better life fade into the oblivion she'll stop squirming and natural instinct to protect her child will be subdued.

It did not happen soon enough for my liking. There was not time to punish her now – I had to get ready for another dull day at the office. The highlight will be a lunchtime visit to a dominatrix, as it was every day. It was with the thought of Mistress that I pulled away from my wife's arse.

TOENAILS

If I could arrive in the carpark early, I could take out a few workers from a different office before stepping into the office and discovering what new idiotic and pointless initiative the board of directors passed overnight. If the police showed up at home wanting to question me, my wife would not tell them anything. That was if she was capable of answering the door – based on the heat coming off her, I was not sure that would be an option for her.

Or I could off the cleaning ladies. Cleaning ladies had exceptionally bad feet; on their wages, pedicures were a luxury they couldn't afford. It would make the morning's work pass quicker.

I was anxious to leave the house. My child's screams shot straight through me this early in the morning, despite not suffering the effects of withdrawal. I did not particularly want to show up at work but not being there or at home could lead the police to me. There were cleaning ladies at every office building. Some even had cleaning men with even grosser feet. Showing up at any one of those would provide me with toenails.

I started my car and left in the direction of work. Automatic reactions caused me to end up in my usual parking spot. The pile of bodies in the corner had not been discovered. I popped a toenail into my mouth and entered the elevator. Today was a whole new world.

...END

Dani Brown

MY LOVELY WIFE by Dani Brown, an excerpt:

TOENAILS

One

Worms and maggots pulse out of the hole in her neck. Big juicy pink night crawlers grow fat with her flesh. I bought them in a shop. The maggots glisten white in the gloom.

She's still alive but barely. The worms and maggots haven't suffocated her. Her chest rises and falls disturbing the flies that have landed on her. Something inside rattles. I might have broken a rib bringing her down here.

My eyes roam up and down her body. She's lost weight. But not enough to see her ribs poking out from beneath her decaying night vest.

Two

I knew I had to have her when I first laid my eyes on her trachea ring. It was a windy day. I nearly walked past her on the street but a sudden gust of wind blew her greying hair off her neck. That was when I saw the hole. Beneath the greying hair she wasn't a plain Jane but a beauty with the most wonderful trachea ring.

I bumped into her accidently on purpose and asked to buy her a cup of coffee to make up for it. With some obvious reluctance she agreed. I can be very persuasive when I need to be. Like when I required her phone number, address and email address (along with her date of birth and mother's maiden name, of course).

I pursued her. I didn't want to frighten her so I wasn't quite relentless. Every time I would pick her up I would give her flowers. A different, more expensive bouquet each time. I'm old fashioned but it worked. Eventually she caved into my advances and agreed to a date.

I took her to the cinema and out for dinner. I paid for everything trying to impress her. I must have because she agreed to a second date. And a third after that. On the third she invited me in. She was innocent and didn't invite me into her bed but she gave me a long deep kiss running her tongue against mine and a glass of red wine before phoning for my taxi.

Three

It wasn't until our fifth date that she let me see her naked. And that was with great reluctance and the lights were dimmed to their lowest setting.

Her grey pubic hairs were properly trimmed like seen on someone younger. I didn't expect that. I thought they would be an untamed jungle. She must have planned ahead. Her creamy breasts were soft with pink nipples staring at the floor. Her armpits and legs were shaved. It seemed all I could do was stare at her and try to see more in the gloom. I hate dimmer switches.

The shadows caught in her cellulite dimples but even they felt smooth when I caressed her thighs. She tried to shrink and push me away but I insisted. I wasn't too forceful, only enough to make her feel wanted.

I led her to the bed and pushed aside the duvet. I wanted her to turn up the light so I could watch her trachea ring without straining my eyes while I pushed in and out of her. But I didn't want to press the issue. It could have frightened her off that first time.

When I stuck my erection in I couldn't tell she had pushed out eight children; although the last one was born nineteen years ago. It felt like I was popping her cherry that late September evening without the messy blood.

The warm inviting hole provided lubricant. I nearly ejaculated upon insertion – it really wasn't what I was expecting. I expected dryness. I thought I might even tear her upon entry without use of Vaseline.

I could tell it hurt her. I could tell by the pained expression on her face and the drops of water in her eyes. She lied and told me that it didn't. She also informed me that she hadn't had any dick since her husband died. She nearly elbowed me in the face reaching for her voice box as I fucked her. I didn't need to know that right that very minute.

Dani Brown

I didn't care that she was in obvious pain. I pushed in anyways, slowly, while asking, "Are you okay?" She claimed she was even after tears dripped down her face, whether that was physical pain or emotions, or a bit of both, I never found out. I didn't care that she was in pain and I probably wouldn't have stopped even if she asked me. I was simply pretending to be a gentle caring lover.

I kissed the tip of her nose and eased out. Then I slowly re-entered. I was as gentle as I could be as I wanted to be invited back for more without degrading myself by begging. After a few minutes of gentle thrusting her raised hips in rhythm (it didn't help though, she should have just laid there like a corpse but I didn't tell her this, I didn't want to be thrown out of her bed).

We took it slow. I wanted her to think it was special. That she was special (which of course, due to that trachea ring, she was). I wanted her to think that I loved her and only her. I wanted her to think it was one very magical moment in time where we became one.

I wanted to stick my tongue in her trachea ring then and there but I restrained myself. That would have resulted in me being pushed off her and to the floor for sure. Then she would have chucked my clothes at me and told me to leave.

The tightness and wetness of her was the only reason I reached orgasm that first time. For someone who was married most of most of her adult life, she was very inexperienced. I imagine her late great husband must've looked outside marriage for his pleasure.

I waited and waited for her to achieve orgasm, like a gentleman should. It never happened. Sex was a chore for her. After pumping away for twenty minutes I couldn't take it any longer and blew my infected load inside her tight dark place.

I pulled out and pulled her into my arms. I kissed the top of her greying head and held her as she cried. Her sobs died away and she fell asleep in my arms for the first time.

Even I managed to doze off. I woke up cold in the middle of the night in an empty bed. I wanted to get under the duvet, roll over and go back to sleep but I knew that if I fancied seeing her and her lovely trachea ring again I would have to go looking for her.

Four

I found her in the kitchen doing nothing except staring out the window. I don't know what she was looking at or for. Maybe a sign of her late husband's approval.

I put my arm around her and gently guided her to the table. Her expression was blank making it impossible to tell what she was thinking. I sat across from her and gripped her cold hands with their dry skin in mine. I rubbed the knuckles trying to bring her back to me. Her skin flaked off and snowed on the polished table.

While her stare was distant I examined the trachea ring with my eyes. I was desperate to examine it with my fingers but the time wasn't right. Skin continued to flake from her hands but still she stared through me and through the wall behind.

I don't think she would have noticed if I started prodding her trachea ring but I didn't want to find out and risk losing her. I don't know how long I sat there rubbing her knuckles. It wasn't relevant. I loved her trachea ring. The rest of her would be mine as well even without my love but it was a price I had to pay.

Five

When I asked her to marry me six months later she agreed. I wouldn't have waited so long but I didn't want to scare her.

Being younger and in better health than her I was capable of getting down on one knee. I had taken her on an evening spring walk along the docks. She needed to rest so sat down on the next bench we came across. She didn't know what I had planned. Maybe she would have sat down sooner if she did, or tried to run away.

TOENAILS

I left her for a few minutes to get her a drink and ice cream. I looked over my shoulder at her sat there as I walked away. The setting spring sun reflected off her sunglasses radiating her pale flesh. Even without the trachea ring she looked beautiful.

She had curled her hair that evening. The greying locks tumbled over her shoulder in little ringlets. It was held away from her forehead by a series of tiny hair clips with butterflies that glittered in the setting sun.

The wind blew off the river making heavy winter coats a must. But it lifted her curls so they tangled with one another. I watched for at least a minute as her hair was lifted, tangled and re-lifted upon my return.

She didn't notice me standing behind her with two ice cream cones and two bottles of water sticking out of my pockets. The wind was too loud for her impeccable hearing to hear my footsteps coming up behind her.

My hands were too full to lift her greying curls and kiss the back of her neck. I wish I hadn't bought myself an ice cream. Her neck was so tasty. But I risked getting carried away each time I touched it.

I walked to the side of the bench. I'm not sure if she noticed me or not. It was always hard to tell what she noticed and what she didn't, after all, she did raise eight kids. She continued to stare at the river but there was a slight curve of a smile on her thin lips. I don't know if she was smiling due to my return or something that happened in that little world she seemed to occupy all by herself most of the time. I didn't care. As long as her trachea ring was in the real world, nothing mattered.

I sat next to her and handed her an ice cream cone without saying a word. She took it without looking at me but instead continued staring at the river. Her eyes didn't follow the seagulls or boats. It confirmed my suspicions that she was lost in her own little world.

Her tongue worked that ice cream cone in a way that made me wish it was my dick. She was too prudish for oral sex – a fact I'll be fixing soon. She would always prevent me going down on her. She never gave a reason. I didn't want to risk losing her lovely trachea ring by shoving my cock in her mouth.

But the way she worked that ice cream. Her tongue savoured every lick. I wanted so much for it to do that to my cock. If I stood up and her attention shifted to me she would have noticed my erection. There was no possible way I would have been able to convince her to duck in the public toilets for a quickie so I pulled my heavy winter coat over my lap and watched the boats.

Seagulls fought over bread dropped by tourists. I'm not sure if she noticed or not. It didn't much matter to me. I wanted something else to watch. She wasn't aware of the way she was eating her ice cream and what it implied. The blood left my cock as I finished my mine watching the seagulls.

TOENAILS

I took the bottles of water out of my pockets and handed one to her. I chanced a look. She had finished at last. My cock hung limply in my pants disappointed that it wouldn't know the inside of a mouth for several months and then only at force so it wouldn't have that nice tongue lapping.

I reached my hand deeper into my pocket. I thought it had fallen out somewhere when I came out empty handed. The back of my mind told me to stick my hand back in. The tip of my finger brushed against the top of a small box. I plunged my hand in further and gripped it with my fist. It left a pink imprint on my palm.

Twinges of anxiety danced across my chest. It was impossible to know what her answer would be. I might only succeed in making her run off. I wanted so much for her to put the ring on her finger, smile and snap a picture for all her friends on the various social networking sites she belonged to. That was all the answer I needed. That was all the answer I wanted.

I would have to ask soon; she'll want to start walking so she could get home before it was too late and answer the phone if her last born called before his night of drink-induced debauchery. I played with the box in my hand in my pocket. She had no idea.

I slipped off the bench and went down on one knee in front of her staring up at her lovely trachea ring.

She must have been able to predict then what I was about to do but she didn't let on.

Whatever world she was in that spring evening wasn't so far removed from the one we share with billions of others. I looked up at her lips to see them curve a little more upwards. I looked up at her eyes – the windows to her soul that were always so guarded, to remember that they were concealed behind sunglasses.

I pulled the box out of my pocket. I lost my voice and couldn't even ask the question. The box sat unopened on my palm. My shaking arm moved over, fingers poised to open but she took it and opened it herself – one of the only times she showed anything even resembling assertiveness. Her neck dropped down as she looked at the ring, obscuring her beautiful trachea ring for a second or so. Her lips turned up further. She took it out and put it on giving me the answer I needed and was so desperate to receive.

Six

I left it to her to plan the wedding. She had already been down the aisle once therefore she had a better idea of how these things worked than I did. I didn't expect the same wedding she had when she was eighteen and walking down the aisle to her childhood sweetheart. I didn't expect her daughters and granddaughters to be dressed in bridesmaid dresses that match their fake tan. I didn't expect a woman of her advanced years to squeeze into a princess gown decorated with LED lights and butterflies, hiding her face behind a veil. She must have been able to read my mind and gave me a wedding I was much more comfortable with.

It wasn't a big church wedding but a nice intimate one at the local registry office with selected friends and family. It was six months after I proposed, in the early winter. We were taking a chance with the weather but I didn't care, I would have been married the next day if she would have allowed it. But she obviously wanted photographs of her second big day, even if they were just taken with her daughter's cheap digital camera.

She wore a lilac trouser suit. The low cut shirt showed off her trachea ring. That was the most beautiful part of her. She wore a silver chain with a floating heart, a gift from me. It drew attention to the most beautiful part of her.

Her greying locks were once again curled and pulled off her forehead with clips that had butterflies on them – just like the day I proposed. But these were new clips to match her lilac trouser suit. The sky was cloudy, otherwise the sunlight would have reflected off the crystals decorating them.

Not even all her children made it to the wedding, even though they were all very close. I never bothered to learn all their names. My excuse to her was that I was terrible with names. It didn't seem to bother her that much. I know it would have really impressed if I learned but not enough for some decent sex.

I have no children (that I'm aware of) to carry on my name once I die. I don't want any. She's too old to give me any – she made that point clear on our first date. My response made her a bit sceptical. She probably thought I would change my mind. Children complicate things far too much for my liking.

My parents came. Both still alive. Both on their third marriages, like it is some sort of competition between them to see who can destroy the most lives. Their spouses didn't bother showing up. They were invited but it was probably for the best.

Her mother was senile drooling down herself and shitting her pants in an old folks home; her father was long in his grave. I thought it might have been amusing to dig him up and bring him but I didn't say so.

The reception was held at a pub. Just small and local. I'm not into obscene public displays of wealth and false affection and love. She knew that it was the little things that counted. The food was nicer than something big booked somewhere fancy. They put on a nice buffet. Everyone seemed to enjoy themselves.

Seven

She even booked a weekend away in the Lake District for our honeymoon. It was in a posh hotel; each room with an ensuite bathroom and room service. I didn't know how she could afford it but I'm guessing she received a discount of some kind or her children pitched in and paid for it. I didn't object. It was lovely.

Now that she was my wife I tried to go down her again but she pushed me away. I poured some lubricant on her instead before pushing my throbbing cock into her still-tight hole. I wanted to insert it into her mouth.

I tried to go into her a bit faster but she didn't like it. She didn't like me biting her nipple either. It took a lot of effort to blow my infected load (hey, I like to spread around diseases, nothing wrong with that). I wanted to but it would have been easier to cum if I sat on my hands while watching paint dry.

She didn't reach orgasm. She never did. If she let me do new things to her she might find that she enjoys them. I think it is highly likely that she never reached orgasm with her late husband either. I pity the poor man for spending so much of his life with her.

Dani Brown

My semen oozed out of her and dripped down her leg when she stood. She wouldn't even let me wipe it off, preferring to shower afterwards by herself, of course. I wanted to lick it but I didn't tell her this.

I sat on the end of the bed playing with my foreskin and sticking my fingers in my mouth to taste her beneath my salted jiz and the chemicals of the lubricant while I waited for her to bathe. I couldn't taste much of her. I couldn't taste much lubricant either. My cum has always had a strong taste of sour milk and salt, like a salty yoghurt.

When she finished she dressed in the large hotel bathroom rather than appear before me wet and wrapped in a fluffy towel. The bright early winter sunlight coming in through the windows probably made her even more bashful than usual.

I continued to eat crust out of my foreskin. She noticed but didn't say anything and left the room. She didn't seem embarrassed by it but it was hard to tell with her. I'm sure she noticed a lot of my more usual habits but never said anything. Because she had only ever been with one man besides myself she might have thought it normal.

I didn't get dressed and follow her. I crawled under the duvet and dreamt of her trachea ring. I dreamt I was inside of it. My entire body, not just my dick. It was weird and vivid. The details have faded now, I wish I had written them down.

Eight

Now she lies on a festering mattress in the fly infested basement. Chained up by both her wrists and ankles. I like the way the chains dig into her flesh. They've rubbed off the skin. Maggots squirm out from underneath them. I like to think they've been eating away at her.

It took some time to get to this point. Years. Two of them filled with three times a week meaningless boring sex – she couldn't even refuse sex on her period; she didn't get one, she went through the menopause. I thought I had a permanent case of blue balls even though I jerked off daily.

End excerpt.

~ It wasn't long before the contents of his mysterious trunk were revealed to her. It was true, they were props, and some of them might even have been used in the circus. Whips and crops, handcuffs, gags and blindfolds. He applied each of them to her liberally and with sadistic abandon. She took to each of them and craved more. This was the other side of Salero, the one he hid, the dark side. Publically, the man loved and craved the laughter and applause of children. But as much as he craved the laughter of children, he also craved the cries and screams of women as they submitted to his own particular brand of sadism. He wielded a whip better than any lion tamer in the business. It thrilled him to watch the firm young flesh of a woman writhe and twist in delicious agony as his ropes bit deeply into them and his crops left myriads of latticework markings on their bodies. Their anguish was his delight.

Dani Brown

~**Rae is her name.** Our support group of embittered and most likely deranged women are going to kidnap, torture, disembowel and finally kill the woman who has ruined all our lives. As foul and as grotesque as she is, she acts like she's Queen of the Bean. Rae, her buck-tooth grin and rosy cheeks of middle age acne reflected winter sun. Straw-like blonde hair obscured by the veil and tiara she enjoyed parading around in. She walked past our window with sickening confidence oblivious to us and our weak tea. Rae. Everything was always about Rae. Was she a princess today, or was she a bride? We wished we could be that delusional and walk around with an air of not giving a damn. Rae believes she is above the pain she has caused. Beyond the whimpering of her victims. Out of reach of vengeance. Our support group of women do not agree. Judgement day is here for Rae.

~Maybe it had started when he was at university. He had a girlfriend in his final year that had gotten him into some weird stuff sexually then she left him for a guy with a bigger cock. The other guy was some gay looking chump with muscles and a tattoo; the pair had died in a car accident and Brian took a dump on their graves after each of their funerals. Fuck the both of them. But after she had left him he needed to fill the void of the newfound enjoyment of sickening sexual practices. Brain had purchased one of those 'real life' sex dolls online. Boy did the thing look real; you could bend it into any position and it came armed with enormous tits, willing mouth and a supposedly real feel pussy and anus. The packaging said to 'just add lubricant' but there was a problem. There was something missing; the smells, the tastes and the feel of real skin. You can't emulate that. So Brian set out to attempt to build a real life sex toy made from real life people.

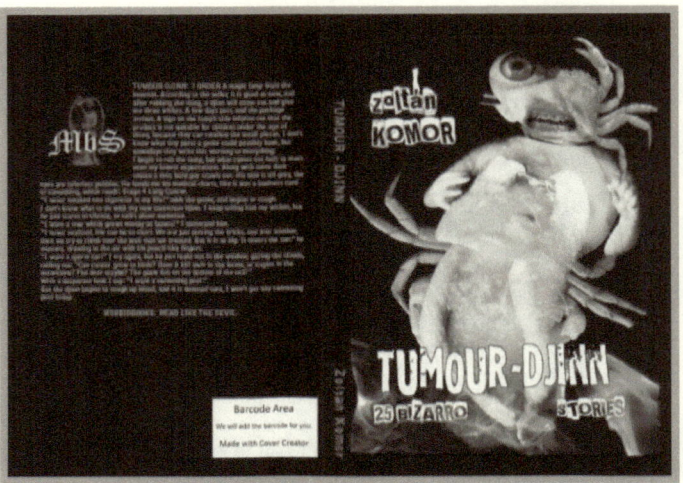

~I ORDER A magic lamp from the internet. According to the seller, it is good as new, and after rubbing the thing, a djinn will come out and give me three wishes. I begin to rub the lamp. Along with some dark smoke a thin, bald guy crawls out. His skin is all grey, the eyes are colorless pebbles.

"I want a tree which grows money as leaves!" I command. "I never realized life can be so short. We are just putting the bricks, one into another, and then we try to climb over the wall that we created. But it is so big. It covers the sun." he mutters. "I want a sports car!" I try again, but he just looks out in the window, gazing the clouds, telling me: "Can cancer grow in birds? Does it kill owls in the forest, or eagles in the mountains? The deer maybe? The giant fish on the bottom of the sea?" With a desperate look I say: "I want a swimming pool." But the djinn begins to cough up blood, and it is damned sure, I won't get any swimming pool today.

~**Keegan is a late-night public access radio show host,** sexual deviant, and militant vegan. He has grown tired of his vegan cause being treated with apathy by the portly, meat-gorging, residents of the small town of Breen Gay, Wisconsin. The time is ripe for Vegan vengeance. Keegan harvests roundworms from a local vagrant and mutates them using chemicals stolen from the meat packing plant. He infests the populace with the voracious, parasitic carnivores. Keegan knows that the only way for the people of Breen Gay to eliminate the parasites is to starve them of meat. It is with great expectation that he awaits the oncoming utopia of Veganism. However, the mutant roundworms will not die easily. The problems for the people of Breen Gay have only just begun.

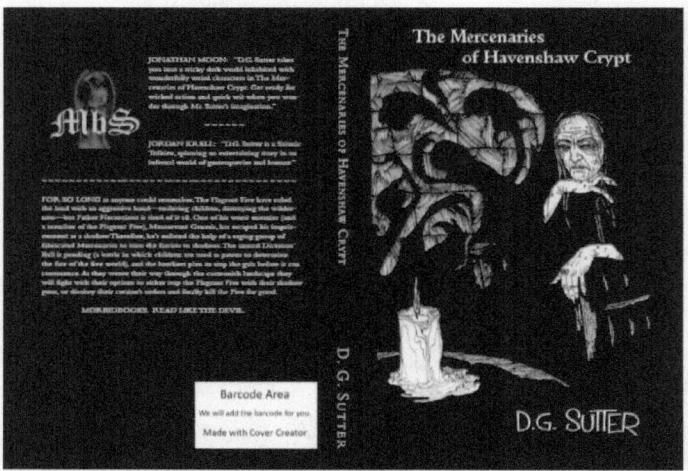

~FOR SO LONG as anyone could remember, The Flagrant Five have ruled the land with an aggressive hand—enslaving children, destroying the wilderness—but Father Necrocious is tired of it all. One of his worst enemies (and a member of the Flagrant Five), Manservant Genesis, has escaped his imprisonment as a shadow.Therefore, he's enlisted the help of a ragtag group of fabricated Mercenaries to turn the fascists to shadows. The annual Dictators' Ball is pending (a battle in which children are used as pawns to determine the fate of the free world), and the brothers plan to stop the gala before it can commence. As they weave their way through the cartoonish landscape they will fight with their options to either trap the Flagrant Five with their shadow guns, or disobey their creator's orders and finally kill the Five for good.

~The hands of the girls were inside of each-others zip front grey boiler suits and they sat in the blood from where Sonny's face collided with the surface. The brunette had a finger smear of it next to her mouth.

"You two sluts put each other down and go tell Moira that Sonny's done. I'm coming in, just got a little business to attend to first."

As the two started to leave the big blond grabbed the shoulder of the red head and pulled her back.

"Not you Fire-Crotch, all this fucking blood has got me going." She started to unbuckle the belt on her camouflage hot pants. "Down you go, bitch!"

~Short stories from the Most Depraved Writer in Print. Dark and twisted tales of exquisite violence, rough tricks, narcotics consumption, evil ghosts and drug-snuffling demons. Evil grandfathers and animal-human hybrid clones. Morbid serial killer stalking night darkened hallways of an unsuspecting hospital. Life underground following the frozen apocalypse. Tales of ancient blood-thirsty vampires and Roman decadence. Enjoy all of the hardcore, dystopic, viscerally violent stories. Not for easily offended mamby-pambies. Dark fiction at its finest.

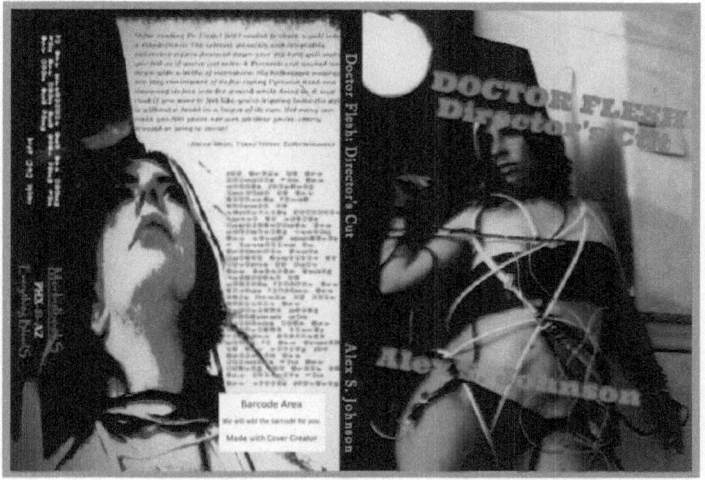

~From Alex S. Johnson, the author of Bad Sunset, Wicked Candy and The Death Jazz, comes a new vision in Bizarro horror. Imagine a TROMA film on meth and acid, one part cyberpunk, one part Franz Kafka, and three parts frankly unsuitable for a sane audience. "Will make you feel as if you've just eaten 8 Percocets and washed 'em down with a bottle of moonshine," says Necro Stein of Texas Terror Entertainment.

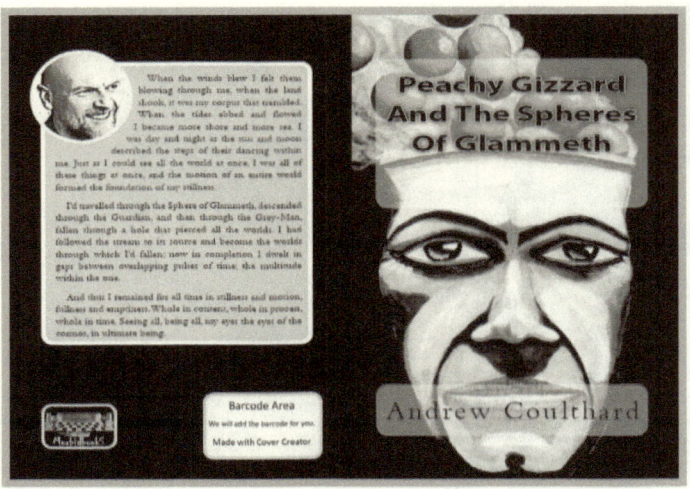

~**When the winds blew i felt them blowing through me,**
when the land shook, it was my corpus that trembled.
When the tides ebbed and flowed I became more shore
and more sea. I was day and night as the sun and moon
described the steps of their dancing within me. Just as I
could see all the world at once, I was all of these things at
once, and the motion of an entire world formed the
foundation of my stillness.

I'd travelled through the Sphere of Glammeth, descended
through the Guardian, and then through the Grey-Man,
fallen through a hole that pierced all the worlds.

~**He had to have her the moment he saw her trachea ring**. Six months later she was his lovely wife. He performed his duties as a husband and she as a wife. He tolerated a house filled with references to her late first husband and the children they had together. He put up with her prudish ways. He waited. He was patient. He planned. He was adaptable. He was rewarded over the course of a week in her basement. He turned his perverse sexual fantasies of worms and maggots and her lovely crusty trachea ring into a gruesome reality.

~A dirty shameful devil of a secret...

Something that two men share. A legacy that will shock you to your very core. One that is created not out of madness, but of the purest desire. Take a vivid journey into the mind of the killer and his biggest fan. Do you believe in evil? See the knife plunge. Lap at the wounds. Do you still? There is no rational meaning or pretty words that will hide away the darkness that the words of this found journal creates. Inside is the real truth. And it can set you free. Watch all you want. Taste what you dare not have.

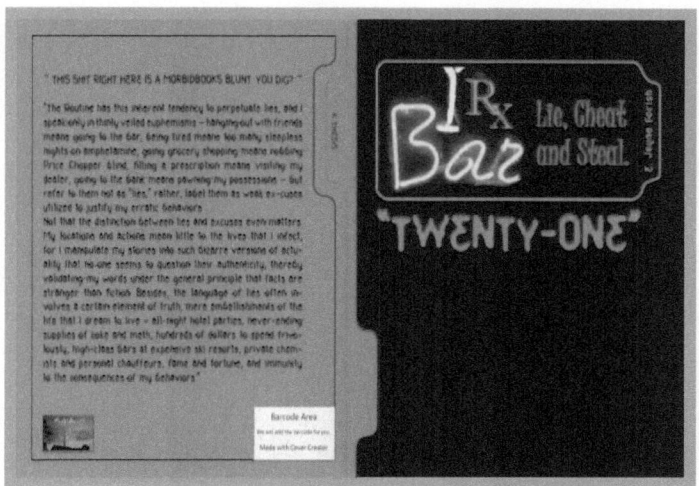

~"The routine has this inherent tendency to perpetuate lies, and I speak only in thinly veiled euphemisms — hanging out with friends means going to the bar; being tired means too many sleepless nights on amphetamine; going grocery shopping means robbing Price Chopper blind; filling a prescription means visiting my dealer; going to the bank means pawning my possessions — but refer to them not as "lies;" rather, label them as weak excuses utilized to justify my erratic behaviours.

~**I'm feeling down and dirty, feeling kind of mean,** so I give those fans my middle finger. Those poor bastards go nuts. My team looks at me in awe. My coach frowns and the opposing one begins to furiously scratch out new plays. I see our opponents and I almost feel sorry for the poor bastards. Their fans can't help them. Their coach can't help them. I'm going to run them off their own track in front of their own fans and there is not one thing they can do about it.

~**Humanity is the devil is a deconstructed nightmare mixing David Lynch and snuff movies.** The plot revolves around a central character, Seth, who is set about a crusade against humanity which, for him, represents pure evil. Through random killings he and his cronies try to accelerate the end of the world, in order to provoke and defeat the Demiurge, the false God that is ruling the earth. As in Burroughs, logical language is replaced here with cut-scenes – sometimes to be taken literally – that plunge the reader into an extreme experience.

Dani Brown

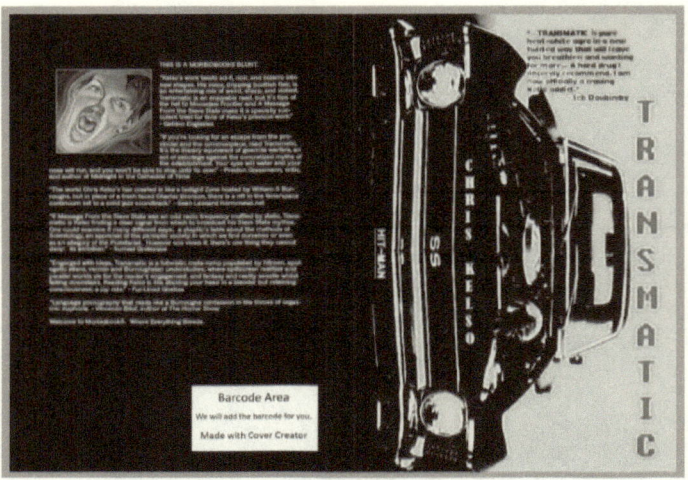

~"As a part-time hitman/ exterminator, Ignius Ellis's dream is to buy a candy-apple red Nova Supreme. In the process of trying to earn enough cash to make his dream come true he gets sucked into the rough world of Visitacion Valley, SF. When the tenants in his apartment complex reveal their various extracurricular activities this take an even more bizarre twist and Ellis soon becomes acquainted with the nightmarish Slave State dimension..."

~That's the last time she gets the bigger worm...

Once their flesh flakes away the angels collapse into puddles of hissing goop and withered petals blow into them hurried along by unseen winds. My spit looses its sweet taste to the black flavor of ash. The glowing birds in the bright orange sky burst into small sparkly novas. The sky itself weeps and tears, streaking down like a ruined painting as the dismal grey of life wheezes back before my eyes. I don't blink; praying silently for one last desperate sensation of the high. Lila feels it too. She writhes on the mattress next to me...

Dani Brown

~Scary as ever.

He looked at her and grinned wickedly, the overcasting shadows of the outer corner of the stone wall, combined with the flickering light above them, created a deadly feature across the side of his face. He sees her lying helpless. He chuckled eerily, and instantly raised his hand. Her eyes widened to the sight of the gleaming sharp knife in his grasp. He even held it up for her to see it better.

She stared up at him and then to the knife, panting in fear. Her heart pounded throughout her body as he chuckled once more saying deeply,

"Oh excellent. I've found you . . ."

~**Within these twisted and perverted pages**, Johnson manages to demolish clichés with a jaded finesse that I've personally never encountered in written form. Another apparent talent is his effortless deconstruction of pop-culture allegories and references as found in his story "Vampussy." No one is safe or spared from his dagger sharp sarcasm and wit.

While not without its flaws, my appreciation for this kind of talent and voice is what made his writing so fun to read, even if he might possibly be out of his ever-loving mind.

Dani Brown

~In Garrett Cook's Murderland serial killers are idolized by society. Their deeds are followed obsessively by television pundits and the adoring public. A subculture has grown up around this phenomena, called "Reap." Laws are created to allow this activity to flourish, including designated "safe zones' where killers can practice their trade without fear of persecution. Fans of the top rated serial killers celebrate each new kill on social media and television. Programs glorify their deeds. The culture of Murderland is violent and mirrors our own violent society and its decadent obsessions.

~Born whole from the rectum of a dying patient, Morbid silently stalks the hospital's hallways, heinously dispatching the most helpless of patients and in the most painfully repulsive of manners. In the meantime, in order to pay for his family and home that includes his ghost step-father Sammy and his pet aborted fetus Chip, Westphal has to ingest mounds of dangerous narcotics to get through his night shifts. Barely hanging on to his Care Tech gig by his fingernails, the last thing Westphal needs is to be accused of Morbid's evil deeds. You, on the other hand, simply seek some solace from all Your diseases.

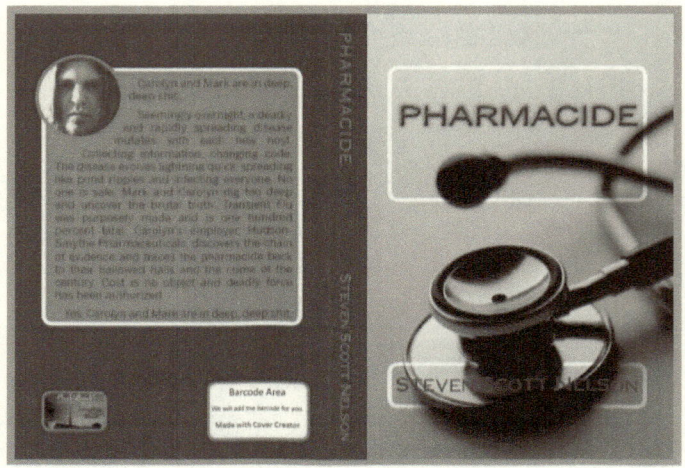

~It looks like Carolyn and Mark are in deep, deep shit... Mark and Carolyn live in an alternate 1989 where Ronald Reagan is on his fourth presidential term. The USA has a rigid, long-standing caste system and abortions were never made legal. Being homeless is a crime that is punishable by imprisonment in Tent City. Most of Mark's ER patients are inmates at this camp and are victims of a new disease dubbed: Transient Flu. This deadly and rapidly spreading disease mutates with each new host, collecting information, changing code. The disease evolves lightning quick, spreading like pond ripples...

~IMMANUEL THE CHRIST has some nerve. Jonah has already lost everyone he loves to Pilate the vampire and his Harbor drug violence. Jonah now trudges through his days staying as high on Plata as possible. He just wants to be left alone while he waits for his turn to die. The Christ has other plans for him. She sends Pedro, to assign Jonah to order the Herod to dismantle the Harbor's Plata trade. Jonah decides to run. But you can't run from God. As Jonah learns the hard way when the 'Edmund Fitzgerald' goes down in rough seas, with the reluctant prophet on board…

~**Five Very Wicked Shorts.** Brought to you with love and blood from The Grim Reverend Steven Rage, the 'Most Depraved Writer in Print'. ~

Through the sheer shock of his presentation, Rage forces readers to consider the alternatives, to look at the garbage in the streets, to see what is swept into the gutters at night right before all decent people awake to see another cleaned up version of the day. Depravity at its finest, but really the stories are loads of fun.

~**Pontius Pilate is cursed to be a vampire.** Life after life after life.~ And for the Plata dealing Pilate, his life is more like a death sentence. His only chance surviving is to keep on selling his monthly quota of Plata. This new man-made narcotic is a potent speed-ball designed to amp up the user, while also numbing the conscience into euphoric oblivion. To nullify the pain. To stifle the torture. To run and to hid from all the anguish inside. PILATE is a drug lord vampire in this re-telling of Christ's final days.

~So I, The Spun Monkey, have returned from running my errands, safe and sound. Having failed rehab once again, The Spun Monkey went ahead and procured myself an 8-ball of crispy, crunchy Columbian Bam-Bam. I chipped, chopped, lined and blasted off with two bigguns up each side. OOH OOH EEE EEE-fuckmerunning- OOH-OOH-OOH, motherfuckers! Monkey be ready... Yes, indeeeeeed.... Having had my jet fuel, I then sat my hairy asshole down at the keyboard and began flailing away. The monkey hopes you dig the fruits of my labors in 'The Spun Monkey's Digest'. And if you not ... well then ... you can go eff yourself, Capitan!

~Following religious folklore, parables, and beliefs, Rage presents the readers with a God who truly is the Shepherd that leaves no sheep behind. While this tale is deeply woven with the intricacies of a dark, drug-infested world ruled by evil forces, this is the story of a lost sheep. All are God's children, even the most foulest of evil creatures who by their own will have become so through their spiritual and physical copulation with the Devil, and as such, in God's mercy, still are given a chance to be saved.

~ CARGO CONTAINS:

1. *Space-wrecked on Venus* by NEIL R. JONES
2. *For All the Marbles* by REV. STEVEN RAGE
3. *Tony and the Beetles* by PHILIP K. DICK
4. *Acid Bath* by VASELEOS GARSON
5. *The Butterfly Kiss* by ARTHUR DEKKER SAVAGE
6. *The Moon Destroyers* by MONROE K. RUCH

FROM SOME OF THE GIANTS OF THE GOLDEN AGE to the darkest of dystopian noir, MorbidbookS SciFi Anthology will take you from hopeful space travel to living hand-to-mouth in the despair beneath the Earth.
Welcome to your future.

~During the height of England's Bubonic Plague an ancient Evil Force strolls into London-Town in the form of a would-be doctor. It could smell the blood from miles away, wanting only to help. At the hospital where he cares for the victims of this Black Death, the ill come to him unimpeded. They arrived and fell by the scores. With the help of his ever-faithful assistant, Sightless Agnes, a most ravenous cares for them all. Eating his way through an entire hospital, he treats them until there is nothing left. Nothing save their empty eye sockets, a few pounds of leeched bleached bones and some bolts of old dried-out flesh-leather parchment.

~New from MorbidbookS: **Where Everything Bleeds** is an instant collector's specimen and a certain stunner. ~ Be the first freak on your block to acquire this singular and unexpurgated exquisite culling of The Grim Reverend Steven Rage's favourite 'meds'. Enjoy this one-of-a-kind vivid look into the twisted mind of The Most Depraved Writer In Print as he captains you through the intoxicating stain of his wicked imagination. Included are numerous Photos, Paintings and Illustrations embellished with dramatic grayscale that enhance these iniquitous and magnificent Dark Fantasy fables.

~Click On Image For More MorbidbookS On Kindle~